HOW TO KISS ON CHRISTMAS MORNING

How to Kiss on Christmas Morning

a sweet holiday novella

JENNY PROCTOR

ISBN: 978-1-967500-14-7

This one is for all the nurses out there.
Thanks for working so hard. You matter.

Author Note

Hi, friends. There are a few scenes in this book that involve a couple of mild medical emergencies. There is no blood. The scenes are not graphic. But I'm warning you just in case! Full disclosure: I am not a medical doctor. (I know! Shocking.) I did, however, research and consult and do my best to portray the scenes correctly. I own I might not have gotten it right for every doctor or nurse. But I hope you'll accept my effort. If the medical stuff bothers you, just focus on the kissing instead. That's really where I shine.

One

I AM A WOMAN WHO LOVES AN ADVENTURE. BUT I HAVE TO admit, right now, even I'm feeling a little nervous.

It's not like I've never experienced snow. I grew up in New York. It snowed all the time. But the mountain roads in Western North Carolina are narrow. And very curvy. And I don't exactly have a lot of confidence in the rental car I'm driving.

Plus, I have no idea where I am. I have never been so grateful for a cell phone connection and the assurance of my GPS, which promises I'll reach my destination within the next seven minutes.

Assuming I don't slide into a ditch before I get there. Or worse, off the side of the mountain altogether.

When I left my brother's house in Harvest Hollow, I

thought I'd have plenty of time to make it to Stonebrook Farm before the snow really got going. But that was, based on the inches covering the road in front of me, a gross miscalculation.

I sigh and slow my speed to less than ten miles an hour. I'm the only car on the road—it's after nine p.m., if the weather isn't reason enough—then turn on my hazard lights and hug the center lane lines, staying as far away as possible from the steep decline to my right.

"You've got this, Megan," I say to myself. "You are brave. You are tough. You are—"

My words cut off when my car veers sharply to the left, crossing through the other lane and onto the grassy shoulder. I do my best to correct my direction, but with zero traction, my steering isn't doing any good. When my left tires tip into the ditch on the side of the road, I finally come to a complete stop, the car tilted enough that I'm leaning uncomfortably against the driver side door.

I grip the steering wheel for several seconds, breathing deeply to bring my heart rate down to a normal pace.

"You're okay," I say out loud. "You're safe." And I *am* safe. A tiny part of me wants to panic, or at least pitch a gigantic tantrum, but a larger part knows that freaking out will only make everything worse.

I close my eyes and do my best to think through my situation logically.

My car is still on, and I have a mostly full tank of gas, which means, at least for the time being, I should be able to stay warm. That's important.

I am also on the side of the road flanked by an incline, the mountain climbing sharply to my left. That's also good. The mountain continues downward on the other side of the road, so had I slid that direction, I would be in much more serious trouble. I am also completely off the road, so if someone else drives by, I'm not in danger of being hit.

Not that I expect anyone to be out in this kind of weather.

But then...if no one else is out in this kind of weather, does that mean...I'm staying here all night?

I look out into the surrounding darkness, and my stomach tightens.

Okay, maybe I *should* start to panic.

At least a little.

I reach for my cell phone, hands trembling as I wake up the screen. I'm not expecting to have a signal—service has been spotty for the last fifteen minutes—but to my utter delight, I have two full bars.

"Thank you, thank you, thank you," I say, still talking to myself. In the eerie stillness of the snowstorm, the sound of my own voice brings a strange sort of comfort.

"Okay, who do I call?"

911? I'm sure they would respond, but in this weather, is it fair to ask first responders to come rescue me? Would they even be able to reach me if the roads aren't safe?

I'm less than two miles away from Stonebrook Farm, but I'm not sure there's anyone there who could help. I pull up the last email I received about my expected arrival. It includes instructions about where I'll be staying and gives me a code to use to unlock the front door, but that's it.

There are extensive instructions about the work I'll be doing once I'm at the farm and a phone number I can call should I run into trouble, but technically, I haven't started working yet. I'm not sure getting stranded in the snow before I've even arrived is the kind of trouble the email is talking about.

I tap my phone against my palm, thinking through my options. I could probably walk. My phone is fully charged, so I'd have at least an hour or two of flashlight before it died. I could walk two miles in an hour.

In the snow.

Carrying my luggage.

Probably.

I glance down at my shoes. My Uggs aren't the best option, but they're better than nothing.

Or maybe I leave my bags for now and come back for them tomorrow when it's daylight and not so snowy?

Still undecided, I pull up my brother's number and call him. He's too far away to help me himself, but he'll at least be able to talk me through my options.

"Hey," Alec says when he answers the call. "Did you make it?"

"Um, almost?"

"What do you mean almost?" my older brother asks.

"So, hypothetically, if you had to decide between walking two miles in the snow or calling 911 because your car slid off the road and into a ditch...what would you choose?"

"Megan," Alec says. "Are you serious? You're stuck on the side of the road?"

"Yes? It's really snowing hard over here. But the good news is I'm less than two miles away from Stonebrook. I think I could probably walk it if I have to."

"Are you okay? Are you hurt?"

"I'm totally fine," I say. "I was going so slow, I don't even think the car is damaged. Just stuck."

"I'm glad you're okay," he says. "But please don't walk anywhere. Just give me a second to fill Evie in."

I listen as Alec summarizes my predicament for my

best friend who is also his new wife. She's the one who got me the gig at Stonebrook Farm in the first place, so maybe she'll have an idea about what I should do.

When Evie first pitched the job, it took me a minute to work out all the connections, but basically, Evie is friends with Summer, and Summer's sister is married to Flint Hawthorne—yes, *that* Flint Hawthorne—and the Hawthorne family owns Stonebrook Farm.

But the Hawthornes are all in Italy for Christmas—a perk of having a movie star in the family—so they needed someone to hold down the fort while they're gone. Answer the phones. Accept deliveries. Host the small family reunion scheduled on Christmas Eve.

My internet research told me that Stonebrook is a commercial apple farm and an event center that hosts weddings, retreats, reunions, that sort of thing. There's also an award-winning restaurant on site that's been featured in food and travel magazines with all kinds of fancy write-ups. It's closed for the season, but seeing it mentioned so many times in my searching, I'm tempted to come back with Alec and Evie when it opens again so we can see what everyone's raving about.

It's a little overwhelming to think I'm going to be in charge of a place that's so nice. Especially when I have zero experience in farming *or* hospitality. But Evie insisted that for this job, I wouldn't need it. I'm mostly getting paid to hang out and call the fire department should anything randomly burst into flame.

Since I just finished nursing school and have zero plans for the holidays, I happily accepted the job offer. A week at a remote farm in North Carolina where I have minimal responsibilities feels like the perfect setup for me to really dig in and study for my licensing exam. The fact that the Hawthornes are paying me so generously doesn't hurt.

Not that it will matter if I freeze to death on the side of the road. I can't exactly take the NCLEX come January if I'm dead.

"Okay, Evie just called Summer," Alec says. "We'll get this figured out."

I sniff and try not to focus on how dark it is outside or how heavy the snowfall has become.

"You're on speaker phone," Alec says.

"Hi, Megan," Evie says. "Okay, I've got Summer on the phone, and she's texting with her sister. They want to know if your GPS is telling you to turn left or right into Stonebrook."

"I can just send you a pin if that will help. But let me check," I say, then I swipe over to my GPS and look at the overview. "Left," I say. "I'm on highway seventeen, one point seven miles from the turn."

"Got it," Evie says.

She's quiet for a beat before she adds, "Okay, they say to stay exactly where you are and don't get out of your car. They're sending Noah to pick you up."

"Who's Noah?"

"He's a Hawthorne cousin," Evie says. "Apparently, he's living at the farm right now."

"Will he even be able to get to me? The roads are barely drivable. That's why I'm stranded in the first place."

"She says he has a very big truck with four-wheel drive," Evie says. "He'll be fine."

I breathe out a sigh. Nothing about this situation is fine. I feel silly. Like I should have been able to prevent this from happening. "Isn't Summer's sister in Italy right now? It's the middle of the night in Italy."

Evie hesitates. "Yes," she finally says. "But you're stranded, Megan. That's a good enough reason to wake someone up."

I drop my head onto the steering wheel and let out a groan. "This is the sister who's married to Flint?"

"Audrey," Evie says. "Yeah. That's her."

"Okay, cool. I'll just be totally chill thinking about Flint Hawthorne waking up in the middle of the night to have a conversation about my poor planning."

"The snowstorm came out of nowhere, Meg," Alec says. "This isn't your fault. I was checking the weather, and I would have made you leave earlier had I thought you'd run into trouble."

"For real, don't worry about it," Evie adds. "Summer says the Hawthornes are all really good people. Oh wait, hang on. She's texting something else." She's quiet for a beat before she lets out a little chuckle. "Okay, she says I should warn you about something before Noah shows up."

"Warn me?" I ask, sitting up a little taller. "About what?"

I can practically *hear* Evie's grin when she says, "Summer says Noah might only be a cousin, but you should brace yourself because he is still Hawthorne-brother handsome."

"What does that mean?" I ask. "There are brothers?"

"Four of them," Evie says. "Flint is the youngest, and Summer says the handsome gene is *strong*. Hang on. She sent me a picture. It's just of the brothers, but it'll still give you an idea. I'm sending it to you."

Seconds later, my phone buzzes in my hand, and a picture pops into my text thread with Evie.

"Oh, geez," I say as I look at the picture. I immediately recognize Flint, since I've seen him in a dozen different movies, but Evie wasn't wrong. His brothers are just as pretty as he is.

I swallow against the sudden knot of nerves making

my throat tight. "So the cousin...Noah. He's this handsome?"

"So Summer says," Evie says.

"The point is," Alec interjects, like he's annoyed we're wasting precious conversation time talking about a group of handsome men that doesn't include him, "he's coming for you. So keep your eyes open and pay attention. Do you have a charger in your car?"

"Yeah, I do. My phone is plugged in right now."

"Good. Keep it plugged in. And keep the car on until Noah gets there."

"What if he doesn't show?" I ask.

"He will," Evie says. "He already responded to Flint. You shouldn't have to wait long."

"Oh, great. So happy it was Flint who texted. I hope he always remembers me as the woman who drove into a ditch. Maybe he could text Taylor Swift so they can laugh about my poor planning. Or—he's friends with Freddie Ridgefield, isn't he? Maybe he'd like to know that I'm the only graduate from my nursing program who still hasn't found a job."

Those last words take me by surprise—or at least the note of irrationality in my tone is surprising. I'm well aware I still haven't found a job, but I'm not sure I realized my feelings about it were so close to the surface.

"Hey," Alec says, his tone gentle. "You're going to find a job. You know you will."

I breathe out a sigh. "I know."

I *do* know. But it probably won't be the kind of job I want, and that's something I'm still struggling to accept.

"What if he can't find me?" I ask, ready to change the subject. My brother gives great pep talks, but he's already given me a billion of them. I don't need another one right now. At least, not about work.

"There's only one road that leads to Stonebrook Farm," Alec says. "If you're on it, he'll find you."

"I'm on it," I say.

"So just stay put. I'm sure he'll be there soon."

"And look on the bright side," Evie adds. "If you *have* to be rescued, getting rescued by a Hawthorne seems like a pretty sweet deal."

Alec grumbles. "I don't think they're *that* handsome."

Evie laughs, and I let myself relax enough to laugh with her. "Not as handsome as you," she says to my brother, her tone softening enough to make my heart squeeze.

Six months ago, I might have rolled my eyes at the exchange, but lately, I'm less annoyed by how much they love each other and more enamored. Maybe even a little envious.

"If he's not there in twenty minutes, call us back."

"I will. Thanks, guys. Give Juno a kiss for me."

"Will do," Alec says. "And Megan?" A hint of mischief creeps into his tone. "When he does show up, you'd better behave."

Two

I T CAN'T BE MORE THAN TEN MINUTES AFTER I HANG UP the phone with Alec that I finally see headlights flashing in the distance, but it feels more like a hundred. I'm not particularly afraid of the dark, and I don't mind being by myself. But I'll still choose company and sunshine at every opportunity, so hanging out in the dark, alone, clinging to the side of a mountain is triggering my discomfort on multiple levels.

I sit up a little taller, watching as the vehicle slowly inches toward me, then pulls to a stop directly beside my passenger side door. There's a Stonebrook Farm logo emblazoned on the side of the truck, and I breathe out a sigh, letting the tension drop out of my shoulders.

I'm more than a little anxious to catch a glimpse of

the Hawthorne-brothers-handsome Noah, but mostly I'm just happy to be rescued.

I turn off my car and climb over to the passenger side, tucking my keys into the pocket of my coat before grabbing my purse and pushing open the door. The car is angled enough that it's difficult to keep the door open, but then a gloved hand appears at the top of the door-frame, holding it steady.

In my semi-crouched position halfway out of the car, my eyes are angled down, so at first, all I can see are his boots. I slowly lift my gaze, trailing up his form. Dark pants. Flannel peeking out from under an unbuttoned Carhartt coat. Trim waist. Broad shoulders. And another gloved hand extended toward me.

"Careful," he says, his deep voice sending a shiver through me. "The ground is slick."

I still haven't looked up to his face. Partly because of my awkward position. Partly because the hot Hawthorne warning left me feeling weirdly anxious.

Which is so unlike me.

I am not the kind of woman who is intimidated by a pretty face. I'm the confident one. The one my girl-friends send across the bar to ask the cute guy if he's seeing anyone and would he be interested in getting my friend's number?

But tonight, I'm all out of sorts.

Maybe it's the snow. Or the half a dozen minutes I spent contemplating what it might feel like to freeze to death. Or maybe it's just that for the first time, I'm in an unfamiliar place and I'm entirely on my own.

I might be the confident one, but that doesn't mean I don't appreciate having my friends standing behind me, holding the safety net to catch me should I crash and burn.

I take a steadying breath and slip my fingers into Noah's gloved hand. Well, I assume this is Noah. I should probably make sure before I climb into his truck.

"You're Noah Hawthorne?"

"Last time I checked," he grumbles. There's a quality to his voice that immediately sets me on edge. He doesn't sound angry, exactly. But his tone is as chilly as the snow collecting on the shoulders of my pea coat.

Once I'm on my feet, I finally lift my gaze.

Oh. Oh, he *is* handsome. Strong jaw. Thick brows over stormy blue eyes. Wavy brown hair and a close-cut beard.

And a scowl that makes my heart shrink inside my chest.

"I'm Megan," I say. "I'm—"

"I know who you are," he says dryly. "Are you good?"

"Am I good?" I repeat. Whatever confidence I usually

have must not like cold weather, because it's all I can do not to shrivel under his icy glare.

"Steady on your feet," he clarifies.

When I nod, he tugs his hand out of mine and tilts his head toward the trunk. "Do you have bags?"

I'm half tempted to say no just to avoid inconveniencing him further. But the thought of my favorite leggings and the oversized hoodie I know are inside my suitcase is too tempting.

"Yeah. Just one...and a backpack," I manage to say. I pull out my keys and use the fob to pop the trunk.

Wordlessly, Noah moves around the car and retrieves my bags, then carries them to his truck, sliding them into the extended cab. He leaves the door open and turns to face me.

I'm still standing beside my car in the triangle of light pooling out of the open passenger door.

"Are you coming?" he asks. "You're getting snow in your car."

I turn and stare at the snow gathering along the edge of the seat like I'm surprised this is happening. But *of course* there's snow in my car. *It's snowing.* And I left the door wide open. "Oh," I say, stupidly. "You're right."

What is wrong with me? I have no idea why this man has me so out of sorts. But the way he's glaring, I can't tell if he's bugged he had to come pick me up or simply annoyed I exist at all.

He has the look of a man annoyed that *anyone* exists. Like all he wants is to go back to his cabin in the forest where he can chop wood and eat beans out of a can and bask in his own solitude.

Either way, he's my ride, so I quickly shut the car door and make my way toward his truck.

Noah waits by the passenger door and watches, his expression almost bored. He offers me another hand, and I almost take it—the truck is very high off the ground—but I'm feeling a little salty over his less-than-friendly greeting, so I ignore it and use the frame of the door to give myself a boost.

Noah tilts his head, eyebrows lifting, and for a second, he almost looks impressed.

See, Mr. Mountain Man? I'm not as helpless as you think I am.

Noah shuts the passenger side door without a word and makes his way around the truck. I breathe deeply while he's gone, an attempt to calm myself and gather some sense of composure, but it backfires, because the inside of the truck smells manly and a little spicy and I'm pretty sure that has everything to do with the man driving it.

I glance his way as he climbs behind the wheel, then

force myself to focus on the road ahead. Otherwise, I'm not sure I'll be able to stop myself from staring. This is ridiculous. It's not like I've never seen men this handsome. I've *dated* men this handsome. But Noah is—I have no idea what Noah is. Or why sitting beside him makes me feel like my mouth is full of gravel.

"I'll come back for your car tomorrow," he says as he slowly eases the truck forward, windshield wipers fighting against the snow. "The weather will have cleared by then."

I lift my fingers to touch the tip of my very cold nose. "Thank you," I manage to say. "And I'm sorry you had to come rescue me in the first place."

He grunts. "It happens."

His icy delivery gives me little reassurance, but I decide to take his words at face value and push on with the conversation.

"So," I say, a little too brightly, "you work at Stonebrook Farm?" I wince as soon as the words are out of my mouth. *Of course* he works at Stonebrook Farm. That's why he's here. Driving a truck with a big "Stonebrook Farm" logo on the side. "I mean, of course you work at the farm," I add before he can answer. "That was a dumb question. I meant to ask what you *do* at the farm."

I'm itching to look at him, to read his expression, but I won't let myself do it. Instead, I lift my eyes upward and stare at the ceiling of the truck, a question suddenly popping into my mind. If the Hawthorne family already has a cousin living on the farm, why do they need me? It's not like they've asked me to do anything particularly difficult. If Noah Hawthorne is capable of driving through the snow to retrieve me, he's capable of answering phones and making sure the Peterson family has enough spiced eggnog for their family reunion.

Noah's quiet for a second, but I feel his gaze on me, and it's all I can do not to look over. Finally, he clears his throat and says, "Whatever they need me to do. Mend fences, tend animals, muck stalls."

Ah. Well, that answers my question, at least. Noah is doing *outside* work. And they brought me on to cover the *inside* work.

"Right. That makes sense." I tug my coat a little tighter around me, then lift my chilled fingers to the warm air blowing from the vents.

"Why does that make sense?" Noah says. "I look like a farmhand?"

"No!" I quickly say. "Not at all. I mean, you *could* look like a farmhand. I don't think there's any kind of rule that says farmhands can't also be h—" I swallow the end of my sentence before I let Noah hear me call him *hot,* but I doubt he's an idiot. He has to know where I was headed. I finally shift my gaze across the truck and see a tiny smirk playing around his lips.

Okay, he *definitely* knows.

I narrow my eyes. Did he do that on purpose? Set me up to say something about his appearance?

The cocky jerk.

"What I *meant* was that it makes sense you're doing farmwork because they hired *me* to watch the desk and take care of things *inside* the farmhouse. Which, they made it seem like there wouldn't really be anyone else around, so I was just acknowledging that if you were doing that sort of thing, they wouldn't need me, so it makes sense that you *aren't*. You're doing outside work instead."

Noah slows and turns onto a wide drive, easing the truck between two massive stone pillars that I assume mark the entrance to the farm. I see a sign, but it's difficult to make it out through the falling snow. "It's a five-hundred-acre commercial operation," he says. "Did you think you were going to be the only one here?"

Five hundred acres? I'm not sure I realized Stonebrook was quite so large.

"Of course not," I lie. Olivia *did* tell me that during the family reunion, catering staff would come in to handle the meal. But that's just one day, and she hired me to be here for a week. I assumed that outside of

Christmas Eve, when the reunion is scheduled, I really *would* be on my own.

"Even in the off season, there's always a skeleton staff to keep things running," Noah continues. He shoots me a look before shifting his eyes back to the road. "Even people who could watch the desk."

I frown, a sense of unease pooling in my midsection. Olivia might have said this would be an easy gig, but she definitely made it seem necessary. Like I would be doing the Hawthornes a huge favor by staying at the farm.

And honestly, it *feels* like a favor. It's December. Christmas is a week away, and I've given up time with friends, time with Alec and Evie and Juno and my parents. That's no small thing, and Noah is making it seem like me being here is completely superfluous. Which, after the ordeal it's been to get here, driving through the snow, getting stuck, having to be rescued, it grates on my nerves to think it's all been for nothing.

"Are you saying I don't need to be here?" I ask. "They're paying me to be here for an entire week. I don't think they'd do that if they didn't need me."

Noah stops the truck in front of an enormous white farmhouse, porch lights glowing through the snow. He unbuckles his seatbelt and opens his door. "I'll get your bags. Try not to slip when you're getting out."

His lack of response has me huffing in indignation as

I climb the porch stairs behind him, gripping the snow-covered railing despite the cold because I will not, under any circumstances, let myself fall in this man's presence.

"Am I missing something?" I ask when I finally reach the top of the steps. A sharp gust of wind blows past, and I suck in a breath. Maybe it's that the adrenaline that's compelled me through the last thirty minutes has finally waned, but I suddenly feel exhausted. Exhausted and *freezing.* "I feel like you're annoyed that I'm here. But it's not like I'm crashing a party. I was hired to be here. Are you just bugged that you had to rescue me?"

Noah's expression shifts, and what looks like a hint of remorse passes behind his navy eyes. He breathes out a sigh. "Let's get you inside, then I'll explain."

Three

I'M MORE THAN A LITTLE CURIOUS ABOUT WHAT NOAH IS going to explain, but I'm temporarily distracted as soon as we step inside the farmhouse.

Holy cow, this place is amazing. My gaze skates past the reception area to an enormous living room full of comfortable furniture and soft lamplight. A fire crackles in the hearth, but it's mostly just embers now, and I have a sudden urge to walk over and put another log on the dying flame.

I would delay the hot shower I desperately need if it meant snuggling up down here. I've never seen any place look so cozy.

"Wow," I say as I take it all in. "This place is great."

Noah nods toward a wide stairway hugging the side of the room. "Your room is upstairs. Kitchen is that way, just past the dining room. You'll have to do your own cooking, but a grocery service brings out the basics twice a week, so if there's anything specific you want, you can add it to the list in the kitchen, and they'll bring it next time they come."

I nod. All of this feels familiar, though I'm suddenly wondering where Noah will eat. If I'll ever run into him in the kitchen—assuming he's staying here too. Which, maybe he isn't? Maybe he's just here to drop me off? "Olivia explained," I say. "I don't mind cooking."

He tugs his gloves off and shoves them into the pocket of his coat before moving into the living room, where he crouches in front of the fireplace and reaches for the stack of wood sitting on the hearth.

I don't want to stand too close to him, but it's hard to resist the pull of the fire.

On the side table next to the couch, there's a book and an empty glass, and it suddenly occurs to me that Noah was probably here, enjoying this room, when he had to retrieve me from the side of the road. *Someone* clearly was, and who else would it be if not him?

I swallow against the sudden knot in my throat. Surely Olivia would have mentioned me sharing the farmhouse with someone else.

Then again, it's a *really big* house. More like a hotel. I

share hotels with strangers all the time, so maybe this won't feel any different?

"So...are you *living* on the farm too? Or just working here?"

He looks up over his shoulder, dark blue eyes sparking in the firelight. "I have a room off the kitchen," he says. "But I won't be in your way."

"I wasn't worried about that," I say a little too quickly, and he lifts an eyebrow.

Just *one* eyebrow. Which makes him look devious and devilish but also annoyingly adorable.

"Fine," I say. "I'm a little surprised Olivia didn't mention there would be someone else here. But it's a big house. I'm sure it will be...fine."

He's quiet for a moment while he stokes the fire, shifting and poking until the flames have sizably grown, then he stands, stepping out of the way and motioning for me to move closer. He pushes his hands into his pockets and watches me, but I don't even care. I'll endure his inscrutable gaze if it means standing right here where the fire can thaw out the chill in my bones.

"Here," he says, holding out his hand. "I'll hang up your coat. You're dripping snow."

I look down, and, sure enough, there are water splotches all over the floor where I'm standing. "Oh. Thanks," I say as I shrug it off my shoulders. He removes his own coat, then walks them both to a coatrack by the front door.

I'm not sure what happened when we came inside, but something shifted with Noah, the iciness to his demeanor melting away to reveal something a little different. It's not like he's suddenly emanating warmth, but he also isn't glaring at me like he wishes he'd left me in the snow.

He walks back to the fire, standing beside me as he holds his hands out to the flames, warming his fingers much like I am. "I'm just guessing here," he says, eyes locked on the flames, "but I'm pretty sure Olivia didn't tell you about me on purpose."

I glance over at him and take in his profile. I don't always go for beards, but his is short and neat and it looks really good on him. "I don't understand."

He lifts his eyes to meet mine, and a spark of electricity races down my spine. "I don't want this to come across the wrong way," he says, "but you don't really need to be here. There are a dozen different employees who could work a few shifts to cover the front desk and host the family reunion. It's easy work. There's no reason to have someone here full time."

"Clearly there *is* a reason, or they wouldn't have hired me," I say. "They offered me a job, and I took it."

"A *job*," he repeats, making air quotes in front of

himself for emphasis, "that I or any other number of employees could have handled. It's a setup, Megan. My family made up a job and gave their regular employees time off so you could come here instead."

My brain temporarily snags on the sound of my name on his lips, but I force myself to focus. "A setup for what?"

He rolls his eyes like he can't quite believe we're even having this conversation. "A setup with *me*," he says, annoyance dripping from his tone.

I frown. "But why would they do that? That doesn't make any sense."

Noah steps away from the fire and sinks onto a nearby armchair. "Because they didn't want me to be alone for Christmas."

I hear myself scoff even as heat floods my cheeks.

A setup?

But Olivia made the job sound so official. And Evie didn't say anything to indicate there was any ulterior motive. Which, she totally would have had she thought the whole situation was anything but straightforward.

I sit down on the chair across from Noah and tuck my feet up under me. "I really don't think that's what's happening here. Olivia listed a bunch of reasons why people needed time off. It all sounded legitimate."

"Then why didn't they tell me you were coming?" he says.

"You didn't know?"

He shakes his head. "Not until this afternoon when Olivia texted and asked me to get your room ready, then added something along the lines of 'she's single, she's beautiful, and you'd better not screw this up.'"

"Oh, wow," I say, my defensiveness deflating. "That does feel pretty pointed."

"And you for sure didn't know anything about me being here?" he asks. "Was your surprise that I'm living in the farmhouse genuine?"

"Completely genuine," I quickly say. "I didn't know there would be anyone else here until I was told you were on the way to pick me up. But I still don't understand why your family would do this." There is *so much* I don't understand, honestly. But I can't think of a question to ask that doesn't feel rude or invasive, so I bite my tongue and hope Noah volunteers something to help me out.

He leans forward and props his elbows on his knees. "My family is in Italy with the rest of the Hawthornes," he says. "My uncle—my dad's brother—is the one who owns Stonebrook. The two families usually celebrate Christmas together. This year, they're celebrating in Italy."

"You didn't want to go?"

"Nope," Noah says simply.

There is an emptiness to his response that makes my heart squeeze in my chest. Normally, I would ask why, but something about his tone—I can tell he doesn't want me to ask. And he definitely doesn't want to tell me.

"Look," Noah says after another long pause, "I shouldn't have been unkind to you, and I'm sorry I was. When Flint called to tell me you were stranded, I was still frustrated about Olivia's meddling, and I half-wondered if you were in on it. But you clearly had no idea what you were getting into, so let's just leave things be and agree to stay out of each other's way. My family is well-intentioned, but I don't need them to force-feed me human companionship. I'm fine being on my own."

I bite my lip and try not to process Noah's words like they're a rejection. He isn't rejecting *me* so much as he's rejecting his family's meddling. *Impressive* meddling, really. Though I'm wondering if it wasn't quite so blatant as Noah is making it seem. The rundown of all the reasons Olivia's employees need extra time off through the holidays sounded real and reasonable. A new grand-baby, an ankle surgery, in-laws visiting from overseas. I doubt she'd outright lie to me.

"I just feel like Olivia would have mentioned..." I say,

but I'm not sure how to finish the sentence. What would she have mentioned?

If she *is* trying to set me up with her cousin, do I really think she would have admitted it?

"What she should have mentioned is that I was going to be here," Noah says. "You're a woman, and you're alone, staying in this big house—you deserved a warning there would be *anyone* staying in with you."

"A warning? Are you dangerous, Noah?" I tease before I can think better of it. It's the kind of flirty thing I would usually say, but I don't know Noah well enough to guess how he'll take it.

His eyes narrow, flashing with something that makes my heart pick up speed.

"Not to you," he says, rather cryptically. "But that doesn't matter. Olivia should have offered you that reassurance. What would have happened had you made it all the way here and let yourself into the house only to find me sitting by the fire?"

"Okay, that's fair," I say. "A heads-up would have been good. Maybe she just forgot? Now that I think about it, Olivia did mention other employees would be around the farm. Just not really...interacting with *me*."

"Then we can still make this work and give us each the holiday we expected," Noah says. "You stay out of my way, and I'll stay out of yours."

I fold my arms across my chest. Whatever softness Noah exhibited seems to have crawled back inside him and died because he's suddenly prickly again. Maybe that's his default setting, and kindness only happens when he really, *really* tries.

If that's the case, it wouldn't surprise me if this isn't a setup at all and Olivia just didn't want to tell Noah she doesn't trust him to host a family reunion with a smile on his face.

I've been in the man's presence for almost an hour already, and he hasn't smiled once.

"Fine with me," I say. "I have a lot of studying to do anyway."

He lifts his eyebrows. "Studying?"

I'm not sure why he thinks he's entitled to answers from me when he's giving me so little information about himself, but I worked too hard in nursing school not to talk about it every chance I get. On the way home from my very last exam, I told an entire subway car that I was officially finished and happily accepted their applause.

"I just graduated from nursing school," I say. "I'm taking the NCLEX in January."

Something passes over Noah's expression, and he shakes his head, huffing out a disbelieving laugh. "Of course you are."

"What's that supposed to mean?" I ask. "Of course I'm a nurse? A college student?"

He stands without answering and walks toward my bags still sitting by the front door. "It's nothing," he says. "Forget I said anything." He picks up my suitcase. "You're in room five—top of the stairs and to the left. I'll carry up your bag. If you need anything else, just look for me. I'm usually around."

I'm good enough at reading people to know that Noah Hawthorne hopes I *don't* need him. Which is fine by me. He can keep his secrets and his angst and his broody demeanor all to himself, and I'll be perfectly happy on my own.

Except, if that's how I feel, then why, when I'm snuggled into my (fabulous) four-poster bed, am I still seeing the flash of his handsome blue eyes and plotting what it would take to finally make him smile?

Four

THE NEXT MORNING, THERE'S A TEXT ON MY PHONE FROM Olivia, apologizing for the ordeal of my arrival. She also apologizes three different times for forgetting to let me know that Noah would also be staying at the farmhouse. She swears she meant to tell me and simply forgot, then she promised I absolutely do not need to worry because Noah wouldn't hurt a housecat.

There is enough humility in her tone that I'm guessing she received a pointed text from Noah, which I appreciate. I really *would* have been freaked out had I shown up at the house and found Noah here without any warning. But Olivia has given me nothing but good vibes, so I take her words at face value and accept her apology.

I have to trust that her intentions weren't malicious, even if she *was* trying to play matchmaker. And I have to believe that she never would have set this up if Noah wasn't a good guy. He may not want to hang out with me, but it's nice knowing I can sleep easily, trusting he doesn't want to harm me either.

I make fast work of showering, but I spend a few extra minutes taming my wavy brown hair into submission and putting on a little makeup. I've learned how to make my brown eyes pop over the years, and for reasons that have everything to do with my new housemate, I put those skills to good use. It's only nine thirty when I make it downstairs, but my car is already parked in the employee lot behind the farmhouse, and there's a fire crackling in the hearth.

Noah clearly had a busy morning.

I glance up at the sky, still laden with heavy, snow-filled clouds, and tug my oversized cardigan around my shoulders.

It's not like it doesn't get cold in New York. New York winters are nothing short of horrible. But something about the remoteness of my location makes the cold feel more threatening. Like there's more danger of it sneaking its way inside the house and icing me over while I sleep.

I go in search of the kitchen, expecting a commercial space, but what I find feels more like a gourmet *home* kitchen than something equipped to feed a dining room full of people. Olivia did mention catering though, so there must be a second kitchen somewhere else. Maybe all the catering prep happens at the restaurant.

Next to the fridge on a small counter, I locate a fancy espresso machine and a regular coffee pot that's half-full of cold coffee.

I open the fully stocked fridge, then turn and run my eyes over the rest of the kitchen. If Noah made himself breakfast, he put everything away and washed every dish he touched.

He could be a fastidious type, but it's more likely he just hasn't eaten yet. Or so I tell myself when I decide to make breakfast for two.

Maybe I'm a glutton for punishment. Or just an utter and complete idiot. But I like people too much not to at least *try* to be nice to Noah. I'm going to be here for a week. I was prepared for solitude, but since he's here and I'm here, it would be stupid for us not to be friends. If not friends, then at least coexisting peacefully and with some degree of kindness.

I'm decent in the kitchen overall, but I'm a pro when it comes to bacon and eggs. And since Evie and I went on a baking spree right before I left Harvest Hollow, I have three loaves of homemade bread in my backpack. They are surprisingly *not* squished after the journey, so I retrieve one and cut it into hearty, thick slices. I'm just about to drop them into the toaster when Noah appears in the doorway.

"Hi," I say brightly. "Are you hungry?"

He frowns, which, hello, that's rude because this breakfast smells amazing. His eyes drift across the two plates sitting on the counter, already loaded with food. "You didn't have to cook for me."

"You're right. I didn't. But I did have to cook for me, and since you already retrieved my car from the side of the mountain, I thought breakfast might be a reasonable way to say thank you." When he doesn't respond, I push my hands into the back pockets of my jeans. "We don't have to eat it together," I add. "It's just food. Eat it wherever you want." I walk back to the toaster and lower in the two slices of homemade bread, then unwrap the butter I left out on the counter to soften, trying my best to seem completely unbothered by the man lurking at the edge of the kitchen.

I should be dismissive. Content to ignore him like he asked me to. But I've never been able to leave riddles alone, and Noah Hawthorne is definitely a riddle.

Why isn't he in Italy with the rest of his family?

Why doesn't he care about being alone at Christmas?

Why is his family so worried about him that they would literally *buy* him company? If that's actually what they did. If it isn't, why does *he* think they're worried about him enough to do it?

"I could eat," Noah finally says, and I glance over my shoulder to see him shrugging out of his coat. Underneath, he's wearing a dark brown henley on top of a white thermal undershirt. He rolls the sleeves up, a white cuff at the edge of the brown, and I catch a glimpse of a tattoo on the inside of his forearm. It's hard not to stare as he moves to the barstool on the opposite side of the enormous island and sits down. He's just so... *present*. Or maybe it's just that I'm so *aware* of his presence. Like my body is tuned to one specific frequency, and he's the only thing I'm picking up.

Noah lifts his gaze to meet mine, and it catches and holds, making my heart climb into my throat.

After less than twenty-four hours and an admittedly less-than-friendly welcome, I can name exactly zero reasons I should be romanticizing this man. Excepting his looks, which are notably extraordinary. But I'm not shallow enough to hang my hopes on a guy just for his looks.

So why can't I look away?

And why do I feel like he doesn't really want me to?

I don't know how long we stare at each other, but something in his blue eyes shifts, then softens.

The toast pops and I startle, one hand flying to my chest as whatever was happening between Noah and me fizzles and dissipates into the air.

Noah clears his throat and I pull out the toast, buttering them one by one before adding them to our plates, then sliding his across the counter.

I don't look up, but I can feel Noah watching me. I wonder if he can sense my nerves, if he's noticing the way my hands are trembling.

Which, *why* are they trembling in the first place? What is even happening to me?

"Thank you," Noah says as he takes the plate. He keeps focused just over my shoulder, like he's intentionally avoiding eye contact. "It looks good."

"Breakfast is easy," I say. "I got good at it during my last rotation of clinicals."

"Yeah? Why is that?" Noah pulls a couple of forks from a drawer at the end of the bar. He motions toward the barstool beside him with a tilt of his head, and I carry my plate around the island so I can sit beside him.

"I worked nights," I say. "Or, I guess *worked* is a relative term since I wasn't getting paid. Either way, my roommates were both nursing majors as well, same year as me, but they were on day shift. We were never home at the same time, so we started planning meals, intentional times for us to be together since our schedules were opposite. Whenever it was my turn to cook, I'd usually been sleeping all day, and I always wanted breakfast food. So that's what I'd make everyone. Eggs, bacon, waffles. I made these killer crepes once. Breakfast always felt easiest."

Noah waits until my fork is in my hand before he takes his first bite. It's a small thing, but I'm pretty sure he was waiting for me. My mother would be impressed by his manners.

Thinking of Mom makes my heart squeeze. This is the first time in a long time I won't be with my parents for Christmas.

Noah takes a bite of toast while I dig into my eggs, but I keep watch out of the corner of my eye, waiting for his reaction.

His eyes widen as he chews. "Where did this come from?" he says through a mouthful of bread.

I can't keep myself from grinning. It's exactly the reaction I expected. "I made that too."

He looks around the kitchen. "This morning?"

"No, I brought it with me. That's actually why I left late yesterday. I was at my brother and sister-in-law's house in Harvest Hollow, and we started baking. I didn't want to leave until everything was finished."

"Suddenly I don't regret having to rescue you quite as much," he says before taking another bite. "It's really good."

I don't know why his praise warms me so much. I've been making bread with my mom for years—she always taught me it was the best kind of therapy—and I'm well aware of how good it is. Noah thinking so shouldn't matter. But a little bit of the tension that's been gripping my chest since I got here yesterday loosens the slightest bit. Mom always says good food can turn strangers into friends. Maybe it'll work for Noah and me.

"Thanks. It's my mom's recipe."

He takes another bite. "You're from Harvest Hollow?"

"Oh, no—that's just where my brother lives. We're from New York, originally. Which is where I was in nursing school. But my brother played for the Appies, and now he works for the team, so he still lives there."

Noah freezes, a forkful of eggs hovering over his plate. "Your brother played hockey?"

Pride swells behind my ribs. "Yeah. Just retired a couple of years ago." I slide my phone out of my back jeans pocket and pull up a recent picture of Alec holding Juno, her chubby toddler hands lifting up to squeeze his cheeks, then hand it over to Noah. "That's him and his daughter. Well, technically stepdaughter. But she's totally his. He's the only dad she's ever known."

I have no idea why I'm talking so much. Why I'm telling Noah such personal details of my life. Maybe it's the nerves. Or a weird attempt to make him want to be friends with me?

I bite my lip as Noah studies the picture, then looks up, eyebrows lifted. "That's Alec Sheridan."

"Yeah, it is. Are you a fan?"

"A bit," he says. "I actually met him once. Five, six years ago?"

"Really? Where?"

He frowns, then shovels in a few more bites of food. I'm not sure if he's embarrassed to have been a fan or if something else is going on, but he definitely doesn't want to tell me about meeting my brother.

"Let me guess," I say, trying to ease the tension. "You wore his jersey to a game and waited outside the stadium so he could sign it for you?"

Noah's mouth quirks up to the side. It's not quite a smile, but it's close. "Not quite," he says simply.

I take a bite of my toast, which really *is* delicious. "You followed his team's travel bus and accosted him in a hotel parking lot?"

Noah huffs out a laugh. "Definitely not."

"Don't laugh. It's happened more than once."

Noah gives me a sideways glance. "I don't envy him that. I would hate being famous."

"Do people sometimes think you *are* famous?" I ask, and he lifts his eyebrows, like he doesn't quite understand my question.

"You look a lot like Flint Hawthorne," I say. "And with the same last name…? I don't know, just wondering how often people make the connection."

He shrugs. "More when I'm clean-shaven."

"Ah," I say around another bite of toast. "Which is why you wear a beard."

He gives me another almost smile. "You're figuring me out."

Hah. Not hardly. But that tiny quirk of his lips does feel like a small victory.

"Okay, so you weren't an overzealous fan. How did you meet Alec, then? Would he remember you?"

"It was nothing," Noah says. "A work thing. I'm sure he wouldn't remember me." He stands from his barstool and carries his empty plate around the island to the sink. "Thank you for this," he says. "It wasn't necessary, but it was delicious."

"What kind of work thing?" I ask, my curiosity officially piqued. "You haven't always worked at the farm?"

Noah's expression immediately shutters closed.

"Only been here a few weeks," he says as he reaches for his coat. "Thanks again for breakfast. Leave the dishes, and I'll do them after I get back. Right now, I need to check on the goats."

Okay, so Noah doesn't like to talk about his work.

Halfway out the door, he pauses and looks at me over his shoulder. "We're supposed to get more snow tomorrow."

I wait for him to add something else, but he just stands there, letting cold air blast into the kitchen.

I fold my arms across my chest, rubbing my hands over my biceps to chase away the chill. "Why does that sound like a warning?"

His eyebrows lift playfully, his gaze sparkling as he shrugs. "Just telling you so you don't try to drive anywhere. I wouldn't want to have to rescue you again."

Something flutters behind my ribcage as he finally dips through the door and shuts it behind him. That almost felt like flirting. *Almost.*

Or maybe that's just wishful thinking?

The truth is, I would *very much* like for Noah to rescue me again. I would like anything that would give him a reason to spend a little more time with me.

Despite my annoyance at Olivia's supposed matchmaking.

Despite Noah's curmudgeonly insistence that we avoid each other.

Despite my pressing need to focus on studying for my exam and not get caught up in Christmas romance fantasies.

It's probably time to admit, if only to myself, that I'm developing a tiny crush on Noah Hawthorne.

Five

I DON'T SEE NOAH FOR THE REST OF THE MORNING, BUT I've got plenty to focus on, so I do my best to put him from my mind.

Several employees come by the front desk to pick up their Christmas bonuses, and the phone rings at least half a dozen times, so overall, I'm feeling pretty useful. I almost wish Noah *was* around just so he could see the *actual, for real* work I'm doing.

And I'm only going to get busier. Tomorrow, I have to decorate the farmhouse. According to Olivia's instructions, there is a storage closet on the third floor where all the decorations live, and I will have plenty to choose from.

I was surprised, at first, when I learned I'd be in charge of decorating, assuming that most places like this probably put Christmas decorations up right after Thanksgiving. But Olivia explained that this year, with the Italy trip looming, the Hawthornes closed the farmhouse to events and decided it wasn't worth the effort to decorate when no one would be here to enjoy it. Except, then the Peterson family called and made a special request to have their reunion at the farmhouse. Their original venue fell through, and they offered to pay triple the usual fee, so Olivia relented and agreed to open the house *just* for Christmas Eve.

The only trouble was that by then, the family was knee-deep in trip planning, and the decorating didn't happen.

So now it's my job.

I make the decision to tackle it first thing tomorrow —the reunion is still days away—then move into the living room to do some studying.

A few minutes after I sit down, the front door opens and Noah steps inside carrying a bundle of firewood. He isn't wearing a coat, so he must not have been outside long.

I watch as he moves into the living room and crouches in front of the hearth to build a fire, much like he did last night, just after my arrival.

"Sorry I didn't do this sooner," he says, glancing at

me over his shoulder. "Had I known you were in here, I would have."

I lift my eyebrows. Did he go outside to get wood just for me? "It's no problem," I say. "I didn't expect it. But thank you."

He nods, then spends several minutes coaxing the fire to life. When it's burning steadily, I assume he'll turn and leave. Instead, he retrieves a book from a side table and settles into the chair across from me.

I frown into my iPad screen.

Noah said he wanted to keep his distance. And this… feels like the opposite of that. We're in the same room. Not ten feet away from each other. And now, I'm so freaking *aware* of him, I'm not going to get any studying done.

Does he expect *me* to leave? Is that what's happening here? He's staking his claim and I'm supposed to scurry off to my bedroom? I hope not, because I was here first, so I absolutely will not—

"Megan," Noah says, and my eyes snap to his.

"Hmm?"

"Don't overthink it," he says dryly. "It's cold outside. The fire is nice. We can share the room like adults."

"Can we?" I say, suddenly feeling salty that he's insinuating *I'm* the problem here. "Because I'm pretty sure it was *you* who requested that I stay out of your way and you stay out of mine."

His jaw tightens, but then his expression shifts and he almost looks chagrined. For a split second, he doesn't seem annoyed with me, but with himself. "I'm sorry I said that," he says. "I was still feeling angry about the setup. If you're comfortable sharing the room, then I am too."

"Of course I'm comfortable," I say. "I actually *like* people."

Noah presses his lips together like he's fighting a grin. "Touché."

I sit back in my chair, battling my own smirk because that exchange with Noah was almost fun.

Still, I'm supposed to be studying, and I am no more capable now than I was before. I might not be worried about what he's thinking, but it's taking all my willpower to keep my eyes on my own paper and not on the gorgeous man sitting across from me.

What's he reading? Does he look like he's enjoying it? Is he looking at me as frequently as I'm looking at him?

Across the room, Noah quietly turns a page.

Okay, probably not.

After considerable effort, I eventually get used to

Noah being in the room. Weirdly, I even start to enjoy his company. I'm not sure I've ever actually done this before, at least not outside of a library, but there's something nice about sharing a space with a person without any expectation of conversation. Not that I would mind talking to Noah. But this is nice too. Companionable. *Easy.*

Just past five o'clock, my stomach lets out a low rumble, so I leave Noah in the living room and head into the kitchen to make dinner. It takes a few minutes of exploring the bounteous supply of ingredients in the fridge, but I eventually decide to make chicken noodle soup. Cold weather always makes me crave soup, plus it will pair well with the homemade bread I brought from Harvest Hollow.

Once all the ingredients are out on the counter, I pause, debating. It's almost impossible to make soup for one person. Noah said I didn't have to cook for him, but if I'm *already* cooking, it only makes sense for me to share.

Decision made, I head back into the living room to let him know my plan. "Hey," I say as I enter the room. "I'm going to make—"

My words cut off as soon as I see Noah because he's fallen asleep.

His book is open on his chest, hands folded over the

top, and his head is tilted back onto the cushion behind him.

Slowly, I make my way into the room. His breathing is steady, like he's really sleeping deeply, so I add another log to the fire, then tiptoe over to his chair.

As carefully as I can, I slide his book off his chest and place it on the sidetable, then drape a blanket over his legs, pulling it up to just below his ribs.

I step away, knowing I shouldn't just stand here staring at him, but it's almost impossible not to. He is no more handsome now than he is when he's awake, but with his face relaxed, completely at rest, there's an air of vulnerability about him that makes something in my heart turn over.

Based on the brief conversations we've had so far, it doesn't feel like a leap to assume that on some level, Noah is hurting. Hurting...or hiding. Maybe a little of both? Otherwise, he wouldn't be here instead of in Italy with his family.

I wonder if he's struggling to sleep. If he has something on his mind, it makes sense that—

Wait. No. I'm not going to play this game. If I keep staring at him, I'm going to write an entire back story for the man, a thousand reasons why I should forgive his surly nature and fall in love with him anyway.

I turn and hurry back to the kitchen, determined to

mind my own business. But once I'm there, I cave and make enough soup for Noah anyway. It's a matter of practicality. It would be a waste of ingredients not to. If Noah wants to eat it, he can eat it. If he doesn't, then he doesn't have to. Simple as that.

As soon as the soup is finished, I help myself to a bowl, eating it with two thick slices of bread slathered with butter.

Noah still hasn't stirred by the time I've cleaned up, so I leave the soup warming on the stove and write him a note, letting him know he's welcome to help himself just so long as he puts the leftovers away.

I figure I'll come back down to check just in case his nap turns into sleeping all night, but when I turn to leave the kitchen, Noah is standing in the doorway.

"You're awake," I say.

He wipes a hand over his face. "Yeah. I didn't even realize I'd fallen asleep." He tilts his head toward the living room. "Thanks for…"

"It was no problem," I say. "I hope I didn't wake you."

He shakes his head no, his eyes moving around the kitchen. "I think the smell of food woke me."

"It's chicken noodle soup," I say. "And there's plenty. I left you a note."

His eyes land on the notecard and pen still sitting on

the counter where I left them. "You don't have to keep feeding me, Megan."

"I know," I quickly say. "But soup is soup. There's always enough for more than one person."

"But I don't want you to think—" He pauses and seems to reconsider his words, but then he never finishes his sentence.

I'm not sure what, precisely, he's insinuating. Maybe he's worried my cooking is some wayward attempt to woo him and he might give me the wrong impression if he keeps eating the meals I prepare. But if he can saunter into the living room and crash my study party and claim it's no big deal, then I can make him soup and leave it on the stove like it's no big deal.

"Of course it isn't." I step a little closer and lift a hand to pat him on his chest. "Don't overthink it, Noah. We both need to eat. The soup is nice. We can share it like adults."

I can't be sure, but as I make my way upstairs, I think I might hear Noah laugh.

***

Once I'm in my room, I retrieve my cell phone from where I left it charging and see a missed call from Evie.

I call her back, putting the call on speaker before I kick off my shoes and climb into bed fully dressed. I look longingly at the fireplace on the far wall and wonder what it would take to get Noah to build a fire for me up here.

Evie answers on the second ring, just as I'm tucking the covers up over my icy feet.

"Hey! How is it?" she asks. She sounds breathless, like she's in the middle of something, but with Juno, it could be anything. That little girl is adorable, but she's a spitfire if ever there was one.

"It's freezing," I say. "I feel like I'm living in a winter wonderland."

"You got more snow down there than we did here, but we're covered up, too," Evie says. "Juno thinks it's amazing, but the cold is making Alec's knee hurt, so I'll be happy when things get back to normal." She grunts, and I hear a *thunk* through the phone.

"What are you doing?" I ask.

"Cleaning out the fridge," she says. "When did I buy tomato juice? This stuff expired six months ago. Ohh! I thought I didn't have any pickles left! Yes!"

I roll my eyes at Evie's inner monologue, but honestly, it makes me happy to hear her rambling on about nothing. She spent too long in a bad marriage, then too long worrying about how to recover after her divorce. She deserves to have silly conversations about pickles and expired tomato juice.

My brother's voice sounds through the phone. "You should let me finish this," he says.

"I'm almost done," Evie says. "And look! I found pickles!"

"Megan, why is she craving pickles?" Alec asks. "I thought it was a myth that pregnant women crave pickles."

I must be on speaker phone now, because both of their voices are coming through the phone loud and clear.

"Not a myth," I say. "Though no one really knows why it happens. It could be the salt. Or the power of suggestion. Pregnant women all want pickles because in their mind, they think they're supposed to."

"I don't care what the reason is," Evie says, her mouth obviously full. "This is the best thing I've ever eaten."

"Hey, I have a question for you," I say to my brother. "But then you have to leave so I can talk to Evie for real."

"Okay, shoot," Alec says. "How are you, by the way? Staying warm?"

"Perfectly warm," I say. "Do you remember ever meeting a Noah Hawthorne?"

"That's the guy who's there with you? The cousin?"

"Yeah. He said he's met you before, but he didn't think you'd remember him."

"Did he say when? Or why?" Alec asks.

"Just that it was a work thing."

"That's weird," Evie says. "What kind of work thing?"

"He didn't say. He isn't exactly the chattiest guy," I say.

"I met with so many people," Alec says. "Could have been anything. Something contract related or maybe an advertising deal of some kind?"

"What about physical therapy or training?" Evie asks.

"I got to know most of those guys pretty well," Alec says. "I'd remember him if that was it."

"Want me to ask Summer what he does for a living?" Evie asks. "I can text her."

"Or can't you just ask him?" Alec asks. "It's not weird that I don't remember someone I met who-knows-where with the team. Why are we acting like this is a big mystery we need to solve?"

"I'm not," I say. "I just asked because I was curious, but I've barely talked to the guy. It's not a big deal."

"Is he nice?" Alec asks, a twinge of something menacing laced through his tone.

"He's very nice," I say. Or, at least nice-ish. "He's mostly keeping to himself."

"Okay, time for you to go now," Evie says.

"What? Why?" Alec says.

"Because Megan doesn't want to talk about this guy with her brother," Evie says. "She wants to talk about him with her best friend."

"But we just *were* talking about him," Alec says.

"That was brother talk," Evie says. "Trust me. There's more."

"Is that true?" Alec asks me.

I hesitate to answer, but who am I kidding? I've been hoping I'd run into Noah all day. And it would be nice to process that with Evie. "It's...a little bit true."

Alec sighs. "Sometimes I hate that you two are best friends."

Based on the sounds that filter through the phone, Evie must lean up and kiss him. "No you don't," she says. "Will you go check on Juno? Her show is probably over, and she needs a bath."

"On it," Alec says. His voice fades as he moves away, but I still hear him yell, "Where's my little girl?"

"Okay, spill it," Evie says. "Was this whole thing really a setup? Summer says she's hearing through the family grapevine that it totally was."

"I have no idea," I say. "Noah thinks it is, but I'm not convinced."

"Are you doing any actual work?"

"I mean, it's only been a day. But yeah. Olivia left stuff for me to do. I'm decorating the farmhouse tomorrow, and I'm answering the phone, and a few different orchard employees came in today to pick up their holiday bonuses, so I'm handing those out."

"Well, that all sounds legit."

"Yeah. But Noah made it seem like there were definitely other employees who could have handled stuff."

"Meh. Whatever. You're there now, and you're going to do a great job. So what's Noah like?"

I tug my covers up a little tighter and breathe out a sigh. "Ridiculously handsome," I say. "And broody and secretive. That's all I've figured out so far."

"Really?"

"Really. I've barely seen him. But…"

"But what?" Evie asks, her tone indicating just how much she's reading into my hesitation.

"But—I don't know. We had this moment when we were eating breakfast this morning and it just—it felt like something sparked or whatever."

"Give me more details," Evie says.

"We were just looking at each other. Nobody was saying anything. But he didn't look away, and I didn't look away, and then my stomach got all twisted and I have no idea. Does that sound stupid?"

"Not at all," Evie says.

"I don't know. I think the whole 'potential setup' idea got in my head, and it's making me see stuff that isn't really happening. Like pregnant women craving pickles."

"Or maybe you just met your future husband," Evie says. "Stranger things have happened. What about after breakfast? Did you see him again?"

"We sat in the living room for like, three hours or something. But we didn't talk. He was reading a book. I was studying. It was all very chill."

"Hmm. That could still mean something. It's better than just full on avoiding you."

"Or it could mean absolutely nothing at all," I say. "Which is the most likely thing. I'm only going to be here a week, so what does it matter anyway?"

"Hey—a lot can happen in a week. And you still might get a job in North Carolina. You have to stop talking like it won't happen."

A pinch of anxiety makes my chest tighten. The pediatric intensive care nurse residency program at the largest hospital in Charlotte is incredibly competitive. Most of my classmates already have jobs lined up, and I've gotten offers from a few other hospitals closer to home. But I *loved* my interview in Charlotte, so I've been holding out, waiting for an offer I'm afraid, at this point, is never going to come.

It would be so perfect. Especially since it's only a few

hours away from Alec and Evie, and I would love to be closer to them with the baby on the way.

"Honestly, Evie, I feel like I would have heard by now if I got in."

"Maybe not," Evie says. "You haven't even taken your NCLEX yet. Maybe you should reach out again. Just to let them know you're still interested and available." Evie stifles a yawn, but it still muffles her words, and that makes *me* yawn.

I glance at my watch. It's only eight thirty, but I feel like I could crash anyway. Nursing school may have permanently ruined my sleep schedule. "I already did," I say. "But I'm not expecting much with the holidays so close."

"Hospitals don't get holidays," Evie says. "I'm sure you'll hear something soon."

I appreciate her vote of confidence, but I've pretty much resigned myself to accepting my second—or even third—choice job. Assuming those are still available. If they aren't, I might be the one who finally ruins the one-hundred-percent-job-placement statistic of my nursing program. Guaranteed work...unless you're me, apparently.

Evie and I chat for a few more minutes, and she sends me a video of Juno talking about her dinner. She's started calling cucumbers *cute numbers*, and it's legitimately the most adorable thing I've ever seen.

"I miss her already," I tell Evie before we say goodbye. "You'd better talk about me every day so she doesn't forget me."

"You know I will," Evie says.

If I wasn't so sure I wanted to work in the PICU, I might apply to work at the hospital in Harvest Hollow just so I could see Juno more frequently. But it's a little too small to have pediatric intensive care, and I'm a little too certain that's what I want my focus to be.

Maybe *too* certain. At this point, I might not have a choice.

Six

I DON'T SEE NOAH THE NEXT MORNING, THOUGH I DO SEE traces of his presence in the kitchen. A full coffee pot. A washed frying pan drying on the counter. A box of apple Danishes with a note scribbled onto the back of the same notecard I used last night.

THE SOUP WAS DELICIOUS. LEFTOVERS ARE IN THE FRIDGE. ALSO, I POLISHED OFF THE LAST OF A LOAF OF BREAD. HOPE THAT'S OKAY, AND THANKS FOR SHARING. HELP YOURSELF TO A DANISH, BUT NOT ALL OF THEM BECAUSE I'M GOING TO WANT ONE IN THE MORNING — NOAH

The note has a slight teasing quality to it that makes

me grin, and the Danish is absolutely delicious. But more importantly, the act of kindness gives me courage because I need to start decorating today, and I'm going to need Noah's help to do it.

Olivia gave me two different options for acquiring a Christmas tree, but both require driving, either to the local Feed 'n Seed where trees are for sale, or all the way up to Thomson's Tree Farm where I can, if I feel so inclined, hike around the mountainside and pick out a tree to be cut fresh and delivered right to the farm.

With the current weather conditions and only a front-wheel drive rental car at my disposal, I'm not sure either is a viable option. Not unless Noah is willing to drive me in his giant Stonebrook Farm truck. Which means I need to go and find him.

With a second Danish in hand, I'm about to head upstairs to grab my coat when Noah steps out of his bedroom and into the kitchen.

His sudden entrance startles me, and I spin around, hand flying to my chest like the gesture will keep my heart from pounding its way out of my ribcage.

"Geez, you scared me," I say.

"Sorry," Noah says. "I wasn't trying to."

"It's fine. I think I'm a little jittery after so much alone time."

He steps over to the counter and picks up a Danish. "You don't like being alone?"

The gesture brings him close enough that I catch his scent, the same one I noted when I climbed into his truck the night he picked me up. It's all I can do not to lean closer, to breathe in an intentional lungful.

Instead, I take a bite of the Danish, which is perfectly flaky and delicious. I wonder for the second time where it came from. As someone who bakes, I appreciate the effort that went into its creation.

"I mean, I don't *hate* it," I say, answering his question. "But if given the choice, company usually makes me happier."

I glance down and notice that Noah isn't wearing any shoes. It's such a silly thing, but something about his socked feet makes a blush crawl up my cheeks. Like it's a reminder of this being a shared space where he lives and relaxes and walks around without his shoes. And now, at least for the next week, it's where I live too.

"Which makes me wonder why you're *here* for Christmas instead of with your family," Noah says. "You came here believing you'd be alone the entire time."

"True, yes," I say. "But this year, my parents are on a two-week Mediterranean cruise to celebrate their anniversary, and my brother will be with his wife's family. They're always happy to have me with them, but holidays with her family—I don't know. They're all so focused on Juno and…I know they love me. But it's hard not to feel like a third wheel."

"Plus the studying you need to do," Noah says.

"Right. Yes. So much studying. And the extra cash I'm earning is a nice bonus."

He takes another bite of Danish. "I'm usually the opposite. I can endure company, but I'm most myself when I'm alone."

"Really?" I say dryly. "I never would have guessed. When I arrived, you seemed so enthusiastic about my company."

His mouth twitches the slightest bit like he's fighting a smile, but he doesn't break.

"Do you have siblings?" I ask, and he nods.

"Three brothers."

"Do they enjoy solitude like you do?"

"They're pretty much the polar opposite of me," he says. "All three of them."

"In what way?"

He seems to really consider his answer before he says, "Let's just say none of them would ever give up a free trip to Italy." He lifts his Danish. "What do you think?"

"They're delicious," I say, accepting the subject

change even if I don't really want to. "Where did they come from?"

"They sell them in the farm store," he says. "I stocked up before it closed for the season."

"Thanks for sharing, then."

"Thanks for sharing your bread."

"There's more if you ever want it." I look toward the two loaves sitting near the toaster. "I won't be able to eat it all before it goes bad, so you'll be doing me a favor. I should probably stick one in the freezer."

"Noted," Noah says. "Thanks."

An awkward silence settles between us, and I shift my weight from one foot to the other. This would be the perfect time to ask Noah for help, but now that I have him in front of me, I'm too nervous to actually get the words out. I can't think of a way to frame them in a way that doesn't sound like a pickup line.

Which is ridiculous. He said he'd be around if I needed help, and I do. So why am I making this so complicated?

I'm about to take the plunge and just ask when Noah clears his throat.

"So, I was thinking..." He pauses and looks up to catch my gaze. "I assume you haven't left the house since you got here, with the weather being what it is, but I thought, if you wanted to get out, you might want to go visit the goats."

"Goats?" I repeat, mostly because I'm pretty sure that was the longest sentence I've ever heard Noah utter.

"Sure," he says, his tone casual. "There was a new one born just a few days ago. She's barely big enough to fill my hands."

I let out a little gasp. "There is a brand new baby goat here, and you're only telling me about it now?"

His lips tick up the slightest bit, and I find myself itching to push for more, to see if I can make him smile for real.

"This is only, what, our third conversation?" he says.

"Fourth, I think? But it's a newborn baby goat, Noah! It should have been the first thing you mentioned!"

"Welcome to Stonebrook Farm. There's a baby goat in the barn?"

"Yes! That would have been perfect!" I love that we're talking like this. That he's letting me tease him.

"Okay, okay," he says. "Point taken. If there are any other baby animals born while you're here, I'll make sure you're the first to know." His tone is easy and playful, and a warm satisfaction spreads through my bones. For a man who comes across as so serious, it's particularly gratifying to make him happy. To see him loosen up a little.

"Thank you very much," I say. "I would appreciate it."

He studies me for a moment before he asks, "Should we go now?"

We. Should *we* go now.

Up until right this moment, I assumed he was only making a suggestion—giving me a way to occupy my own time. But going to the barn *with him*—that has a different vibe.

Is he asking because he wants to spend time with me? After all that talk of preferring solitude? Or does he just feel sorry for me? Things didn't seem so bad last night, and he *did* leave a box of Danishes for me. He's either had a change of heart or he really likes my bread and doesn't want to feel guilty for eating it all.

Either way, after the welcome he gave me—or *didn't* give me—an actual invitation to spend time with him feels like a big shift.

"You know what? Some other time," Noah adds when I fail to respond.

"No, no! Now is good," I quickly say. "Just give me a second to grab my coat." I pop one last bite of Danish into my mouth and head for the stairs.

I won't say no to *any* baby animal, but I'm self aware enough to own that the speed that takes me up to my room and back down again, coat and scarf in hand, doesn't have anything to do with livestock, newborn or not.

The air is chilly when we step outside, the sky a crisp bright blue. Noah warned me we were getting more snow, but it doesn't look like more than a few inches fell. "How long will this stick around?" I ask as we walk toward the barn. I can just see it in the distance.

"Not long. We're supposed to get another six inches tomorrow night, but it's supposed to warm up after that, so it'll melt pretty quick."

"Do you think it'll impact the reunion?" It's the twenty-first now, and the reunion is scheduled for Christmas Eve. If we're getting more snow tomorrow, it seems unlikely the roads will be clear.

"It might," he says. "But I doubt it. It should all melt in time."

"That seems totally wild to me," I say. "When it snows in New York, it sticks around forever."

"We might be in the mountains, but we're still in the South," Noah says. "Cold comes in snaps more than spells." There's a slight Southern twinge to his accent that I've never noticed before, and it makes me smile.

"What?" he says as he looks over at me.

"Nothing." I push my hands into the pockets of my coat, wishing I'd thought to grab my gloves. "You just sounded Southern when you said that. I haven't noticed your accent before."

He shrugs as we approach the barn door. "It comes out more when I'm in Silver Creek. Or when I'm talking to my family."

"I get that," I say. "I don't think I sound like I'm from New York, but my college roommate is from Brooklyn, and when we're talking, she pulls an accent out of me that I don't usually have."

"Do you live in the city?" he asks.

"I was there for nursing school. But I grew up in White Plains, about an hour north."

The heavy barn door creaks and groans as Noah slides it open, and the smell of hay hits my nose. "I've never been to New York City," he says as he motions me into the barn.

I step through the door, happy to find that the air inside is significantly warmer. Across the barn, a goat with big white ears pokes its head over a stall door and lets out a welcoming *meh-eh-eh-eh-eh.*

"You should visit New York," I say. "It's a great place. Great food."

"So I've heard," Noah says. I wait as he closes the door, then we head toward the goats together. "Do you think you'll stick around there?" he asks. "For work?"

"I hope not," I say. "I mean, I loved it for school. And

my parents are still in White Plains. But...I don't know. It's so busy. I think I'll be happier somewhere smaller."

"Yeah? Like where?"

"My top choice is a hospital in Charlotte—Northvale General. It's close to Alec and Evie, and they have a PICU nurse residency program that's one of the best in the country. The program is super competitive," I add, "and I probably would have heard by now if I got in. But...I don't know. Maybe I'll get lucky and someone else will drop out to make room for me."

"That's a great hospital," Noah says, something in his tone giving me pause. He sounds like he's speaking from personal experience.

"You know it?"

We stop in front of a large stall with half a dozen goats inside. They're all crowded around the door, looking at us like they fully expect us to have pockets full of treats. I'm suddenly sorry I didn't bring anything to give them.

"I lived in Charlotte for a while," Noah says. "So I know the area pretty well."

I wait, expecting him to add something more. To tell me that's where his family is from or where he went to school. Charlotte isn't far from here, so it wouldn't be that unusual. But to mention the hospital specifically feels odd. Does he know it's a good hospital because someone was sick? Or because *he* was sick?

"Is that where you grew up?" I finally ask when he doesn't add anything else.

"No," Noah says. "I grew up just north of Asheville."

"Oh. That's not too far."

I wait again, leaving the door wide open for Noah to volunteer more information, but then he steps inside the goat pen, and I can tell we're leaving the topic of Charlotte behind us.

I can't call it annoying that he's so obviously withholding information. It's not like I'm entitled to any of his secrets. But the fact that he *has* secrets makes me insatiably curious, and it takes everything in me to keep myself from asking more questions.

At least until I see him pick up the tiniest goat I've ever seen in my life.

Once I see Noah cradling her against his chest, I'm not thinking about his secrets at all. The goat leans up and nuzzles his beard, then lets out a tiny *meh-eh-eh-eh*. He scratches under her chin with his free hand. "That's a sweet baby," he whispers. "You're such a good girl."

The words are obviously not meant for me, but heat pools in my belly anyway. He's being so gentle, so tender with her. It's a side of Noah I haven't seen before—and

I'm not sure I could have imagined it had I tried. But here we are.

Swooning over a large man holding a tiny goat was not on my Christmas bingo card this year, but I'm about ready to write it in over every single space. Because honestly, what else could possibly compare to this?

"You want to hold her?" he asks, though he doesn't look particularly excited about giving her up.

It's a toss-up. Watching *him* hold a baby goat is an experience that might actually rival holding one myself. To see someone so broad and strong and masculine be so gentle—it's the very best kind of drug.

Still, I don't stop him when he lowers the coal-black newborn into my arms. She settles right in like she was born to be held like this, then leans up and nuzzles my neck with her nose.

"Oh, my gosh," I whisper. "Could she be any more perfect?"

Noah steps closer and scratches the top of her head. "She's the third one born since I've been here, but it still feels like a miracle every time I see it happen. It's hard not to love them when they're this tiny and new."

"That feeling was almost enough to make me do labor and delivery instead of PICU," I say. "It's pretty amazing when it's people too."

He scratches the newborn under her chin. "I bet goats are easier patients."

I laugh. "No birth plans and no stressed-out dads-to-be. I think you're probably right about that."

"Have you thought of a name yet?" a voice asks from somewhere behind me. I turn to see a blond woman walking toward us from the opposite end of the barn. She's wearing a Stonebrook Farm jacket, jeans, and thick rubber boots.

"Not yet," Noah says to the woman, then he looks down at me. "This is Kelly, the farm manager here at Stonebrook. Kelly, this is Megan. She's who Olivia hired to keep an eye on the office while everyone is in Italy."

"Nice to meet you," Kelly says. "Olivia told me you'd be here. I've been meaning to stop by and say hello, but with all this weather, I haven't had the time. It's a lot of work weatherproofing a farm. You're connected to the family, right? Someone's cousin? Or...sister, maybe?"

"Just a friend," I say. "Or, a friend of a friend, really."

Kelly smiles. "Well, a friend of a friend is a friend of mine. I appreciate you filling in. I've never seen Olivia so worried about covering everything while she's gone."

I give Noah a pointed look. "Thank you," I say, not even trying to hide the smugness in my tone. I *knew* Olivia actually needed me to be here. "I'm so happy to help out."

Noah's phone rings before he can contribute to the conversation, and he pulls it out, giving the screen a quick glance. "I should take this," he says. "I'll be right back."

I smile at Kelly as Noah walks away. "Honestly, I'm happy to hear you say I'm needed. I've been feeling a little weird about being here. Especially with the weather. If the Christmas Eve reunion is cancelled...I don't know. I just don't like feeling extra."

She narrows her eyes at me. "Did someone say something to make you *feel* extra?"

I wince the slightest bit. "No, no! I'm sure it was nothing."

She gives me a pointed look. "Megan."

The woman is too perceptive for her own good. "Noah *might* have said something about the job just being a cover for some sort of weird Christmas setup. He thinks his family didn't want him to be alone for Christmas."

Her eyes widen. "He told you that?"

I nod. "The first night I arrived."

She huffs out a laugh. "Perceptive of him to piece it all together."

I frown. "Wait. So it *is* a setup?"

"No, no," Kelly says. "You're definitely needed. But Olivia did hire *you* on purpose. As opposed to, say, my mother-in-law, who would have been happy to help out but probably would have been a much less fun houseguest for Noah." She shrugs like it's no big deal. "Two things can be true at once. You're needed. Fair and square. But after what Noah has been through, no one's going to pretend like he doesn't also need a friend."

"What he's been through?" I ask, and Kelly grimaces, like she's suddenly realized she's said too much.

"Honestly, it's perfectly understandable in his line of work," she says. "I shouldn't have even mentioned it because I'm sure he's going to be fine."

Kelly's candid response is more than I expect, and I'm not sure how to respond.

What has Noah been through? And what is his line of work?

A part of me wants to ask. With a little prodding, I'm guessing I could get Kelly to talk. But a bigger part feels like that would be betraying Noah's trust somehow. It doesn't feel right to ask for information he might not want me to know.

Still, if I don't figure this guy out soon, the *not* knowing might eat me alive.

Noah's mood is subdued when he comes back into the barn.

"Everything okay?" I ask.

He nods as he slips his phone back into his pocket. "Yep. All good."

I'm not sure I believe him, but I probably shouldn't be trusted. Not when my brain is imagining a raft of possible secrets and heartaches big enough to make all these people worry as much as they are.

"Ready to head back?" he asks.

I nod and give the tiny goat one more scratch behind her ears before letting Kelly lift her out of my arms. "You should name her Noel," I say, "since she was born so close to Christmas."

The goat lets out a tiny bleat, and Kelly smiles. "I think she agrees."

Seven

"You're quiet," I say as we make our way back to the house.

"I'm always quiet." Noah's tone isn't defensive at all. Just matter-of-fact.

"True," I concede. "But you're more quiet than normal." It almost feels like a silly thing to say. Have I known Noah long enough for us to have a normal? But there's definitely something different about him now. He's more contemplative. Like his own thoughts are consuming so much of his energy, he doesn't have any left for the outside world.

We walk in silence for several steps before he says, "That was my mom on the phone."

"Ah. Tough conversation?"

I brace myself, ready for him to shut me down, but

he surprises me when he says, "Not really. She's just worried about me. And even though she tries not to say it out loud, I can tell by the tone in her voice that she is."

"I mean, she's in Italy and you're *here*. Can you blame her?"

Noah shoots me a sideways glance. "No, I guess not."

"You could still go, you know," I say. "Catch a flight. You'd be there before Christmas."

"Nah," he says. "I've got responsibilities here." His steps slow as we approach the back stoop of the farmhouse. "Besides. If I leave, who will help you decorate for the reunion?"

I spin to face him. "You'll help me? I've been meaning to ask you, but I wasn't sure you'd want to. Or would have time with all the..." I glance back toward the barn. "The farm things."

"Farm things?"

I roll my eyes. "Shut up. I don't really know what it is you do around here. Animals? Apples?"

"Roadside rescues?" Noah adds, his lips lifting into a tiny smirk.

"You aren't going to let me forget that, are you?"

A crisp winter wind swirls around us, and Noah pushes his hands into his coat pockets. "I do a little of everything," he says. "But it's Christmas. The farm things can wait."

"It's Christmas?" I repeat as I follow him up the steps to the back door. "What suddenly thawed the ice around your grumpy heart?"

He holds the door for me. "The text from Olivia threatening bodily harm if I didn't offer my services might have something to do with it."

I wait to respond until we're both inside the kitchen, the door closed against the quickly decreasing temperature outside. "And here I thought you were determined to do the opposite of what Olivia wanted." I take a step toward him. "Refuse to be set up. You stay out of my way. I stay out of yours."

I'm close enough now that he has to look down to meet my gaze. "I did say that," he says. "But then I tasted your homemade bread and decided some things are worth the sacrifice."

I fight a smile, leaning forward the slightest bit. "So this is about the bread."

"Yep."

"Nothing else?"

His lips twitch. "Nope."

"And you're okay with me monopolizing your *entire* afternoon with Christmas things?"

His jaw tightens like he might be reconsidering, but then he nods. "Whatever you need."

I settle back onto my heels and consider his offer. I

need his help, so I'm not going to argue. But I can't quite make out his intentions.

Noah seems like a man at war with himself. He must want to spend time with me; otherwise, he wouldn't be standing here volunteering his help. And he wouldn't have asked me to go see the goats. No matter what he says about Olivia, he's clearly a man who makes his own choices.

But he's also holding a huge part of himself back. He's here. But he's not *all* here. And I wish I could figure out why.

"Perfect," I finally say. I take a huge step backward, needing a breath of air that doesn't smell like Noah. "I'll definitely need help moving the decorations from the storage closet upstairs. But the biggest thing is getting a Christmas tree. Will you drive me?"

He turns and looks through the window toward the parking lot like he's checking to make sure the giant Stonebrook Farm pickup truck is still there.

"I'd do it in the rental car, but with the roads, I'm not sure that's a very good idea," I add.

"It's definitely not. Where were you wanting to go?"

"Thomson Tree Farm. Or, if that won't work, the Feed n' Seed in Silver Creek. But..."

"Let me guess," Noah says. "You want to pick one out at the tree farm?"

"Is it Christmas if I don't get to pick out the tree?" I ask.

His expression shifts, another almost smile that sets off a tiny explosion of fireworks in my belly.

"We could get up to Thomson's in the truck," he says, "but not everyone has four-wheel drive, and it's a pretty steep climb between here and there. I'm guessing they're closed if only to keep people from trying to make the drive."

My shoulders drop. "The Feed 'N Seed then?"

"They're probably open. They almost always are." Noah hesitates, his eyes looking over my shoulder and past the house. "But we might have another option." He pulls out his phone. "Let me just ask Liv if she minds."

I like the way he calls his cousin Liv. Like they're friends too, not just family. It was only ever me and Alec growing up, which was totally fine. He and I have always had a great relationship. But I love the idea of a big family like this. Of cousins you know well enough to randomly text and have it be no big deal.

"Wait," I say, suddenly realizing something. "If you have three brothers and no sisters—does that make Olivia the only girl? In the whole extended family?"

Noah nods. "Yeah. Tough gig, right?"

"There are no other cousins?"

"Not on the Hawthorne side," Noah says. "I think she

has some on her mom's side, but it's just my dad and Ray on the Hawthorne side. Eight boys and Olivia."

"Where does she fit in the lineup? Age wise?"

"She's the youngest in her family," Noah says. "And she's younger than me, but she's older than the rest of my brothers. Flint and I are the same age."

My skin prickles with awareness at the mention of the movie star. Noah says it so casually, but it's not lost on me that if my tiny Christmas crush on Noah were to turn into something real and I actually started dating him, I would probably meet Flint Hawthorne.

I've never been particularly obsessed with the actor. It's just weird to hear him mentioned and know Noah actually knows him. That he grew up with him.

"Megan," Noah says, cutting through my thoughts, and I swing my gaze to him.

He's wearing an amused expression that makes heat climb up the back of my neck and gives me the distinct impression that wasn't the first time he's said my name.

"What?" I say, feigning an innocence I don't really feel.

His mouth quirks up to the side. "You were thinking about Flint, weren't you?"

"What? No. Of course not."

He lifts an eyebrow. "Liar."

I scoff. "I'm not lying. I wasn't!"

His expression doesn't break.

"Okay, fine. I *was*. But I was only thinking about how weird it must be to have someone that famous in the family."

Noah pockets his phone. "Probably no different than it is for you to have a brother who played pro hockey. He's just your brother, right? He has fans, people obsessed with him. But he's still just Alec to you."

My brother isn't even in the same stratosphere as Flint Hawthorne. The man won an Oscar last year. But I understand what Noah is saying.

"Are you ever going to tell me how you met my brother?" I ask. I have no idea where I suddenly get the courage to ask. Maybe it's because Noah seems like he's teasing me. And if he's comfortable enough to do that, then I'm comfortable enough to tease him back.

"Are you changing the subject so you don't have to admit you have a crush on my cousin?"

"I do *not* have a crush on your cousin."

"He was *People Magazine*'s sexiest man alive."

"Sexiness is subjective," I say. "Are *you* changing the subject so you don't have to talk about your work?"

Something flashes behind Noah's eyes, and his jaw flexes before he raises a hand and runs it across his beard. "I *work* at Stonebrook Farm," he says, like it is not up for debate, then he breathes out a sigh. "Which is why I know exactly where to find you the perfect Christmas tree."

I don't miss the way he says *you*. Like he's doing this for me, in particular.

Something flutters inside my ribcage, a pulse of longing that's growing stronger and stronger every second we're together. It's maddening to feel so much attraction when there's still so much I don't know. But for now, I'm content to let him win.

I take a step toward him, dropping my defensive posture and opening my hands, making it clear I'm accepting defeat. "Okay. Then let's go get a Christmas tree."

Eight

I EXPECT NOAH TO LEAD ME TO HIS TRUCK, BUT IT TURNS out the perfect Christmas tree is within walking distance of the farmhouse. We take a slight detour past a toolshed for Noah to retrieve a wide-tooth saw, then we walk to a hillside maybe fifty yards behind the house. We stop in front of an enormous fir tree, its wide green arms stretching toward the sky.

I don't know a ton about fir trees. We always used a fake tree growing up because it was what we had, but this one looks like it came out of a children's picture book.

Perfect Christmas tree shape. Perfect deep green needles.

"Are you kidding me right now?" I say as we

approach the tree. "This is just...growing out here? Right beside the house?"

Noah clears his throat. "It isn't here by accident."

I look around the hillside and notice that there is only one tree like this one. "No?"

He walks to the tree and circles it, then leans in and pushes on the trunk like he's testing its sturdiness.

"I was maybe eight or nine," he eventually says, "and my family came to the farm just like we always do. Uncle Ray took me and Flint up to Thomson's to pick out a tree. They had a giant tent up with dozens of trees inside, but this one was in a planter near the entrance. It was only a couple feet tall, and it wasn't for sale—it was just there for decoration—but I got it in my head that I wanted to buy it." He shakes his head and breathes out a little chuckle. "Flint and I argued about it. He wanted the tallest tree he could find and didn't understand why I was so hung up on this one."

"Why were you?" I ask, and Noah shrugs.

"Who knows? Maybe I just liked being contrary. But I think a part of me liked that it was still alive. It had roots, dirt. It could keep on living even after the holiday was over."

"That's a nice thought," I say. "So they let you buy it?"

"Eventually," Noah says. "I don't know what Uncle

Ray said or if they tried to refuse. I just know we brought this tiny two-foot tree home right beside the big one we bought to go inside the house. It sat on the front porch, and I tended it the whole time we were here like it was my pet. Flint thought I was ridiculous, but after New Years, Uncle Ray brought me out here, and we planted it together."

"And you think I'm going to let you cut it down *now*?" I ask, because honestly, has he lost his mind? The tree has to be ten feet tall at this point. With a history like that, he can't really want to cut it down.

"I wouldn't," Noah says as he steps closer to the tree. "Except, it's not thriving anymore." He motions me forward and points toward the base of the tree, bending down to push the branches aside. "Down there close to the root, there are a couple of soft spots on the trunk. I had an arborist come out and look at it last week. It's not a good sign."

"There isn't anything you can do?"

Noah shakes his head. "Unfortunately, no. It hasn't gotten any taller the past few years. Apparently, we aren't at a high enough elevation for it to thrive. The ground is too wet. The air is too humid. It's probably lucky to have lived this long."

"So you're saying it's dying?" I ask, and the thought makes me sad.

"Something like that," Noah says. "It might hang on a few more years. But I don't think it's happy here."

I rub my hand across one of the branches, finally noticing the dry, brown needles clinging to the tips of several boughs. There aren't many, but for a tree that's still in the ground, I'm guessing there shouldn't be any.

"Noah, I don't need a Christmas tree today. Or even one at all. If the weather doesn't clear, the Peterson family might not even come for a reunion. I don't want to cut down your tree for nothing."

He looks up at the tree, one leg propped onto a rock, the saw hanging loosely from his fingers. Out here on the hillside, with his canvas jacket and his beard and a freaking saw in his hand, his already *very* masculine vibe has practically doubled.

I've been in the city the past three years, so I haven't seen this level of rugged in too long. Overall, it is *really* working for me.

"It wouldn't be for nothing," Noah finally says. "Even if the Petersons don't come, it's still Christmas. I'll still be here." He holds my gaze and lifts his shoulders in a tiny shrug like it almost pains him to admit the next part. "And you will too."

The words make me surer than ever that somewhere beneath Noah's broody exterior, there's a man who doesn't want to be alone for the holidays after all, no matter what he told his family.

Feeling empowered by his admission, I cross the distance between us and push up on my toes, my hands curling around his forearm as I press a kiss to his cheek.

The skin above his beard is warm, despite the chill in the air, and I find myself lingering, my nose brushing against him as I breathe him in.

"Thank you," I say softly. "This really means a lot."

As I lower back onto my heels, the loose snow shifts under my feet and I lose my balance, but I only wobble a moment before Noah steadies me, hooking his arm around my waist and tugging me against him.

My hands lift reflexively, and I press them against his chest.

"Careful," he says, his voice low and a little raspy.

I tilt my head upward, and his face is *right there,* his blue eyes intense and focused wholly on me.

Just like it did the other morning in the kitchen, Noah's gaze wraps around me, making my skin heat and my face flush. I bite my bottom lip even as my gaze drops to *his* lips. They're so close—close enough for me to see the flecks of amber in his beard and notice the tiny freckle just below his lip.

Noah's hand tightens against my back, his fingertips

pressing against my skin with new intention, and for a split second, I think he might lean down and kiss me. He licks his lips, his head shifting forward until his nose touches mine, but then he clears his throat and shifts away.

His hand slips from my back and grips my elbow, like he wants to make sure I won't topple over before he lets me go completely.

I drop my hands from his chest and step back, willing the heat in my cheeks to dissipate. Maybe he'll think I'm just flushed because of the cold. In truth, it's taking all my willpower to stand here normally and not melt into a puddle of embarrassment.

Except—I'm not sure I *should* be embarrassed. He clearly wanted to kiss me. All the signs were there. He even leaned close enough for our noses to touch.

So why did he back away?

Disappointment pricks painfully as I step away and force myself to look anywhere but at Noah.

Over the past few days, Noah has annoyed me and frustrated me and confounded me. But he has also intrigued me and puzzled me and left me wanting more. *A lot* more, apparently. Because I've never been so disappointed to *not* be kissed.

"I should..." Noah motions to the tree with a slight tilt of his head and lifts the saw.

"Right. Good," I say. "Thanks for..." I wave my hand

up and down my body as if that's explanation enough for why I couldn't seem to stay on my feet. "Catching me."

Noah offers me a wry grin. "Is that what happened?"

I lift my eyebrows playfully, at least appreciating he isn't going to pretend like nothing happened. "Unfortunately, it's *all* that happened."

At first, I'm not sure Noah hears me, but as he leans down and positions the saw on the trunk of the tree, I catch a glimpse of a smirk that makes me think he absolutely did.

Nine

It's possible, as we drag the Christmas tree back to the house, that I fantasize a tiny bit about Noah and me decorating together, listening to music, drinking eggnog while we hang ornaments on the tree like we're in some sort of holiday romance movie. He *did* say he was available to help.

But after the *almost* kiss on the side of the mountain, I won't be surprised if he makes his excuses the minute the tree is inside.

But he doesn't do it. Once the Fraser fir is secure in its stand, we work together to move all the decorations downstairs, then he builds a fire in the fireplace and gets to work weaving lights through the branches of the tree.

I turn on some Christmas music, and before long, I am fully engrossed in the magic of turning the Stonebrook Farm farmhouse into a winter wonderland. Olivia said I could keep things low key, but honestly, once I start, it's hard to stop.

A tiny village with snow-capped houses. Garland trimmed with twinkle lights. Ornaments in every color of the rainbow. There are scented pinecones that smell like cinnamon and a beautiful nativity scene and a set of hammered copper Christmas trees that I set up on the hearth where they reflect the flickering firelight.

The afternoon isn't exactly movie-worthy. There is no kissing under the mistletoe or snuggling by the fire. But we *do* exchange a few lingering looks. And every time he moves past me, he touches my arm or my shoulder or the small of my back.

Every time, fire shoots across my skin, crackles of energy that heighten my awareness of him. The longer we're together, the more he starts to relax, enough that I start to wonder if I actually *do* have him figured out. He's quiet and a little bit intense. He appreciates his solitude, and he doesn't like small talk. Which means he's happy to have people think he's grumpy because that means he's often left alone. But the more I get to know him, the more I'm seeing his kindness. He's thoughtful and intentional and a really good listener. I find myself telling him things I've never told anyone—about what it felt like when my best friend married my brother. About the bittersweetness of losing a little piece of them both when they fell in love with each other. We talk about my parents and my friends in New York, and he tells me about summers on Stonebrook Farm, chasing pigs and climbing mountains and eating apples right off the trees.

Somehow, spending time with Noah feels new and exciting and utterly unexpected while also feeling warm and familiar, like I've known him all my life.

I have no idea how both things can be true at once, but with him, they absolutely are.

Finally, I hang the last ornament on the tree, then stand in the middle of the room, making a slow circle as I admire our work.

It's perfect. So perfect, I have to hope the weather allows the Petersons to come.

If not, well, Noah was right. This is where I'll be spending *my* holiday, too. It's nice to have things looking so Christmasy.

"It looks great," Noah says from the entry into the dining room. He disappeared into the kitchen a few minutes ago, saying something about warming up the spiced cider in the fridge. "As good as it usually does."

"Does it?" I turn to face him and find him leaning against the door jamb, arms folded loosely across his chest. He looks relaxed and happy and achingly handsome.

"If you wind up hating nursing, you might have a career in holiday decorations."

I grin. "I'm not going to hate nursing, but it's nice to know I have a backup."

"Do you want some cider? It's almost warm."

I can already pick up the scent of cinnamon and cloves, and it's making my mouth water.

"Yes! Definitely. But I'm going to go wrap some garland around the porch posts first."

Noah nods. "Let me turn off the stove, then I'll come out to help."

I carry the box of lighted garland outside and make quick work of wrapping the railings, but there are columns on either side of the stairs and I would love to continue the garland up each one. I might have to find a ladder to do it.

Unless—

I test the sturdiness of the railing. It's wide and flat and feels perfectly solid. Definitely sturdy enough to hold my weight. I hold the garland between my teeth and use both hands to hoist myself up.

It takes me a second to find my balance, but once I'm steady, I stand upright and carefully wrap the garland around the left porch column. There's even a tiny hook at the top, like this has been done before and the hook is there for just this purpose. I secure the end of the garland around the column with a satisfied sigh. "Perfect," I say.

Then my foot slips and I lose my balance, falling forward off the railing and onto the snowy front lawn with an audible *oof.*

I'm not sure if it's better or worse that I fell forward into the snow instead of backward onto the porch. The snowy ground is a couple of feet lower, but the snow at least cushioned my fall.

At least, I think it did.

I lay perfectly still, cataloging the many parts of my body that hurt. I landed on my left hand, and my palm is stinging and cold, and my hip aches, the damp snow already seeping through my pants. But maybe that's the worst of it?

I shift and try to sit up and...*oh, no. I am definitely not okay.*

Sharp pain radiates up my shoulder, and a wave of nausea washes over me. I roll onto my back and close my eyes, willing myself not to throw up. This is definitely the throwing up kind of pain.

I breathe slowly, tears pricking my eyes as the shock of my fall wears off enough for me to realize how badly my shoulder hurts. Everything else pales in comparison.

Did I break it? Or break my arm, maybe?

I swear softly, then the front door clicks open.

"Megan?" Noah calls. I hear the moment he sees me, because he swears too, then he races down the steps.

In seconds, he's crouching beside me in the snow.

"What happened? Are you hurt?"

"I fell off the railing," I say without opening my eyes. "I was hanging the garland."

"Stay perfectly still, okay?" he says gently. Then his hands are moving over me. Touching my legs, my arms, brushing my hair away from my neck and sliding his palms across my collarbone. When he moves outward to my shoulders, I wince and suck in a gasp.

"I think I broke something," I say. "It really hurts."

"Can you wiggle your fingers for me?" Noah asks as his hand slides down my left arm.

I do as he asks—his confidence makes it very easy to trust him at the moment—but I'm only marginally successful. I feel my fingers pressing into the snow, but they are tingly and uncomfortable, like they've fallen asleep from too little blood flow. On impulse, I lift my arm to look at my fingers, except...I *can't* lift my arm.

At all.

"Noah, I can't move my arm," I say, fighting a rising sense of panic that's only making my nausea worse. I really, *really* think I'm going to throw up. "Can you take me to the hospital?"

"Just breathe for me, okay?" he says. "You need to keep breathing." His hands are still on my shoulder, gently prodding, like he's feeling for something specific.

"What I *need* is to go to the hospital," I say. "I'm the one with medical training here. And I'm pretty sure I've broken something."

"You didn't break anything," he says, his voice calm. "At least, I don't think you did. But you did dislocate your shoulder."

I don't know why Noah would know, but as soon as the words are out of his mouth, I sense that he's right.

He stands and shifts so he's crouching behind me, his hands moving to my neck and back to my collarbone. "No pain through here?" he says, prodding gently. There is an efficiency to his movements that gives me pause. It does not seem like this is the first time Noah has asked these questions.

"No, I don't think so," I say. "My shoulder is the only thing that hurts."

He comes back around to my side. "Can you put your good arm around me? We need to get you out of the snow."

I do as he asks, because he's right. I wasn't wearing a

coat, thinking it wouldn't take long to hang the garland, and the snow has already soaked through my clothes.

"Noah, I need to go to the hospital," I say. "If I *did* dislocate my shoulder, a doctor will be able to pop it back into place."

Noah is quiet while he scoops me into his arms and tucks me against his chest, then carries me into the house, making it look far too easy. I don't exactly mind being in his arms, but it's hard to really enjoy it with my shoulder throbbing so painfully.

He deposits me on the couch next to the Christmas tree with my bum shoulder facing out, then he grabs a throw pillow to put behind my head and another to prop under my feet.

"I appreciate this," I say, wondering if my earlier words just didn't register. "But I really *do* need to go to the hospital."

He sinks back onto his heels. "I'll take you if that's what you want to do," he says. "But if you're okay with it and you trust me, I think I can take care of you here."

I narrow my eyes and study Noah's face.

I *do* trust him. But trusting that he won't ax-murder me in my sleep while we're sharing the farmhouse is not the same thing as trusting him to take care of my medical needs. Though I'm not opposed to the idea of him taking care of me. I maybe even like the idea. A lot.

But my arm is hanging from its socket like a limp pool noodle. This feels bigger than just *taking care.*

"You could pop my shoulder back into place?" I ask. "How would you know how to do that?"

He sighs and rubs a hand across his face, like it's causing him physical pain to have this conversation. "I know how to do it because I'm a doctor." He hesitates, storm clouds passing behind his expression. "I *used* to be a doctor. But I can do this for you. If you'll let me."

For a split second, I almost forget how badly my shoulder hurts.

Noah's a doctor? That at least explains the way he was examining my body outside.

"I don't understand," I say. "If you—why are you—?"

His gaze softens, and he lifts a hand to my face, his thumb brushing across my cheek. "It's not important," he says gently. "Will you let me help you? There's no reason for you to sit here in pain."

I nod and relax back onto the cushions as another wave of nausea washes over me. I close my eyes and take a steadying breath, then open them to meet Noah's warm gaze. "Okay. I trust you."

He nods once, then he gently adjusts my body, I assume shifting me to give him easier access to my shoulder. "Can we take this off?" he says, tugging at my sweater. It buttons down the front and I have a tank top underneath, but the question still makes me blush.

I mentally chide myself for having any kind of reaction. Noah's a doctor, and right now, all he wants to do is...doctor me.

I nod, fumbling one-handed with the buttons, but Noah gently moves my hand away and takes care of them himself. It shouldn't be sexy. Nothing about the pain I'm feeling right now is sexy, and he's being completely professional. But Noah's quiet focus, the surety of his movements, his calm confidence—those things *are* sexy, and I find myself captivated. Or as captivated as I can be with my shoulder hanging out of joint.

"Sit up for me?" Noah says. He slips an arm behind me one more time and helps me sit up so he can slip my sweater off my shoulders and pull it out from under me. "It's a complete dislocation," he says. "Anterior. Which is the most common type of dislocation. It means the bone has shifted—"

"Forward and downward," I say. "I know what it means."

He nods appreciatively. "I forgot I was working on a nurse." He takes hold of my arm, and I close my eyes, bracing myself for what's coming.

"Try to relax for me," Noah says, his voice soothing, and I take a deep breath.

"Good. Do that one more time."

I breathe in and before I even realize what's happening, Noah applies pressure to my arm, shifts, pushes, then *pop*.

The relief is immediate, and I breathe out the air I'm still holding in my lungs.

"How does that feel?" Noah says. His hand slides down my arm, moving it gently, tugging it upward, then pushing it back again, then moving it in one slow rotation.

"Better. So much better," I say.

He nods. "Good. You're still going to be sore. Tylenol. Ibuprofen. You can alternate every four to six hours if you need it. And I'll see if I can rig you up some sort of sling for the next few days to keep you from overusing it. Actually, let me get you some pain medication now—"

I reach out and stop him before he can leave, grabbing hold of his sleeve.

He turns back, crouching beside me one more time. I reach for his hand, and he takes my fingers, holding them gently between his palms.

"Thank you," I say. "That was much easier than going to the hospital."

His face is unreadable, but that's not much of a surprise. If I have a glass face, showing every emotion, right now, Noah's is like a thick slab of granite.

"You're welcome," he says, giving my fingers a squeeze. I am not disappointed when he doesn't drop my hand.

I rub my thumb over the top of his knuckles. "You're a doctor," I say simply.

A shadow passes behind his eyes, and he takes a deep breath. He doesn't pull away, not physically, but I still sense his retreat. "Not anymore," he says, his voice thin.

"I don't understand," I say for the second time.

He shrugs. "It's not that complicated."

It's *obviously* complicated, but it's hardly my place to push him.

"What was your specialty?" I ask, hoping my use of the past tense *was* will give him enough room to answer.

His jaw tightens. "Emergency medicine."

"Intense."

"Yep," he says curtly, and I feel a sudden need to chase away the distance that's growing between us. To make him look me in the eye and tell me what's hurting. Because there's definitely something. A wound just under the surface that's making his expression hollow.

He finally tugs his hand away and pushes himself to his feet. "I'll be right back," he says.

Noah returns after just a few moments, but he isn't really present. He's kind, courteous, solicitous, concerned for my comfort. But he's treating me like a patient. Not a friend.

He warms up the leftover soup and bread I planned to eat for dinner but doesn't accept my invitation to eat with me. He tends the fire, adding wood whenever it's needed, but he doesn't sit down. He doesn't *relax*. And he doesn't make eye contact even once.

The longer it goes on, the more my heart aches. I already like him enough that I want to know more of his story. But mostly I just want to make him feel better.

It's not like nursing school gave me a ton of experience, but I've been in hospitals enough to understand how taxing it can be. How much it can drain you. And to be in the ER—that's a level of intense all its own.

I'm finished with my soup and gazing into the fire when Noah appears one more time. I thought he might have already gone to bed, so it's a surprise to see him. Wordlessly, he crouches in front of the hearth and adds another log to the fire, then sits back on his heels and looks at me. "Do you need anything else? Or can I help you upstairs?"

"I'm not ready for bed yet, but when I am, I think I can make it on my own. My legs still seem to work okay." I offer him a teasing smile, but his face doesn't crack at all.

Apparently, the Doctor Hawthorne version of Noah is all business, all the time.

"You'll probably have some bruising tomorrow," he says. "Just take it easy."

I nod. "Yes, Doctor."

He flinches, and I immediately wish I could call back the words. "Noah, wait," I say as he turns away. "I didn't mean…" My words trail off, and he pauses and turns back, looking at me over his shoulder.

"I'm sorry," I say. "I didn't mean that to be mocking."

He pushes his hands into his pockets, eyes on the floor. "I know you didn't."

"I'm not going to push you to talk about it," I say gently, crossing my fingers that I'm not about to make things worse. "But if you *wanted* to talk about it, I've been told I'm a very good listener."

"There's nothing to talk about," he says a little too quickly. "I *was* a doctor, now I'm not anymore. It isn't a big deal."

I study him. The set of his shoulders. The visible tension in his jaw. "Respectfully, your body language is telling a different story."

Something flashes behind his eyes. "Respectfully, it still isn't any of your business."

I can't keep myself from wincing at his words, and

something like remorse passes over his expression. But he doesn't take them back.

"Got it," I say softly. "Understood."

Noah doesn't say anything else. He just breathes out a sigh and turns and walks from the room.

When I came to Stonebrook Farm, I expected to spend Christmas alone, and I was okay with that. But after spending a few days in Noah's company, his absence doesn't feel like solitude; it feels like loneliness.

Like my heart is missing something it just figured out it wants.

Ten

THE PROMISED SECOND ROUND OF SNOW STARTS FALLING sometime around midnight. I'm still awake, trying to watch a movie and keep my mind off the broody doctor downstairs. But it's hardly doing much good. Even though it's the kind of movie I would normally love, I can't follow the plot, and I keep having to pause and rewind to figure out what's happening.

Noah's a doctor.

That's why he scoffed when he found out I just graduated from nursing school. He thinks Olivia chose me on purpose. Maybe because we would have something in common?

But what is he doing here? Not that it's hard to imagine why he might have quit. Especially if he was in emergency medicine. There are countless resources designed to help medical professionals deal with trauma and death and loss, but he wouldn't be the first doctor to step away, if only for a time.

Then again, it can't be all that uncommon for doctors to shift from regular practice to something else. Teaching, or research, maybe. But Noah was very specific when he said he *wasn't* a doctor—not anymore. That's not the kind of language you use when you're shifting gears to focus on research.

I breathe out a sigh and reach for the remote. The couple on the TV screen who I thought were cousins just kissed. I've been struggling to follow the plot, but I didn't think I was *that* far off. Maybe I'll try again tomorrow when I'm not feeling so distracted. Though with Noah around, I'm not sure that's possible.

I lift the remote and aim it at the TV, but before I can turn it off, the screen goes black on its own, and the lights overhead flicker and then go out.

I hold my breath, waiting, hoping it's just a fluke. A temporary glitch. But thirty seconds turn into a minute, then five minutes.

The power is officially out.

I toss my covers aside and pad across the plush carpet to the window. It's snowing pretty steadily, adding an additional layer of white on the already blanketed ground.

At the edge of my vision, a beam of light flickers, and I crane my neck to watch as someone moves across the edge of the lawn, a flashlight dancing across the ground. It has to be Noah, since he emerged from the house, and I wonder where he's headed, but I lose sight of him when he turns into the trees.

I sigh and head back to bed, where I retrieve my phone from the nightstand, using the flashlight to take myself to the bathroom so I can pee and brush my teeth. I'm already wearing my pajamas, but there isn't much to them. Just a thin chemise with tiny spaghetti straps that only falls to my mid-thigh. I debate for a moment on whether I should add a few more layers. I tend to get hot while I sleep, but I love the weight of a lot of blankets, so I usually opt for tiny clothes and heavy covers. There's definitely a slight chill in the air, but I think I'll be fine once I'm in bed, so I climb back in and pull the covers up to my chin.

I glance at my phone one last time, then set it on the nightstand and turn off the screen, plunging myself into total darkness. My phone battery is only at seventeen percent, which is enough for right now, but I'll have to figure out a way to charge it tomorrow if the power doesn't come back on. I could sit in the car, at least, and juice it up that way.

I stare into the darkness and listen to the eerily quiet

house. It's funny how quiet *quiet* really feels when all the background noises of a power-filled house are gone. No central heat. No hum of the refrigerator. Just the occasional creak of an old house.

Except—that sounds like more than a creak.

It sounds like footsteps.

My hands tighten around the covers as my heart starts pounding in my chest.

Has it been long enough that Noah would already be back inside? The footsteps sound heavy—like they belong to a man wearing boots. And...are they coming up the stairs?

It has to be Noah.

But what if it isn't? What if it's someone else entirely?

It takes about three seconds for my brain to imagine a hundred different scenarios, all ending with my ultimate demise before a knock finally sounds on my door.

"Megan?"

My shoulders relax as I take a relieved breath. It's Noah. *Of course* it's Noah. "Hmmm?" Despite my certainty that there is not an ax murderer on the other side of the door, my voice still sounds strangled and cracked. I clear my throat and try again. "Yes?"

"I have wood," Noah says, voice muffled.

I push up on my elbows, not sure I heard him right. "Um...you have *wood*?" I say through a giggle.

There's a long pause before Noah says, "Very funny. Are we eighth graders now?"

"You started it," I say as I toss my covers aside, sucking in a gasp as the quickly chilling air reaches my bare legs.

"I have split logs to build you a fire," Noah says pointedly, though I can hear traces of humor in his tone. "You might get cold with the power out."

After the way we parted a few hours ago, it's nice that he's here. Even nicer that he's willing to joke with me.

I glance in the general direction of the fireplace. It's too dark to see it, but I know it's there. And a fire really would be nice.

"Just a sec!" I call, then I reach for my phone and turn on the flashlight one more time. I have a robe somewhere, and if I'm answering the door for Noah, I definitely need to find it.

It takes a minute. Apparently, I packed like a drunk chimpanzee because nothing is where it should be. After digging ineffectively for what feels like three hours, Noah's boots scuff against the floor outside the door. "Everything okay?" he asks.

"Yes!" I call as I start tossing clothes out of my bag. "Just looking for—got it!" I grab the robe and shake it out with one hand, then toss my phone onto my bed so

I can pull it on. The movement sends a sharp pain through my shoulder, and I suck in a gasp, then adjust and try again, being more careful. Something isn't right—the robe is tugging in weird places—but I've already made Noah wait for too long, so I stumble my way toward the small beam of light shining under the door.

I bump my hip against a chair on the way, letting out a muffled *"Ow,"* but I arrive otherwise unscathed. I take a steadying breath before swinging the door open, but the extra oxygen does little good, so my heart is still racing when I look up to make eye contact with Noah.

He's holding a small lantern, and it casts a circle of warm yellow light into my room.

"Hi," I say as I take in his hulking, shadowy form. He's fully dressed, still wearing his heavy winter coat, and his shoulders are dusted with snow. "Sorry. I was looking for my robe."

His eyes drop to my body for the briefest moment, and I resist the urge to flinch. To tug my robe tighter or fold my arms around my middle. I might be wearing a lot less than I was the last time he saw me, but I'm still decent.

His mouth quirks up the slightest bit on one side, his eyes fixed somewhere on my midsection. "Good thing you found it."

I look down and...*oh, sheesh.* My robe is on, but one side is completely twisted and the left arm is inside out.

"Wow," I say. "I genuinely have no idea how I managed to get it this wrong."

"It sounded like it hurt," Noah says with something that sounds like concern.

"A little," I say. "I wasn't thinking about being careful. Just trying not to keep you waiting."

Noah wordlessly sets down the lantern and lifts his hands toward my waist. "May I? I don't want you straining your shoulder."

Well, this *definitely* isn't going to help my heart rate, but I nod my head anyway. He gingerly unties my robe, then slips it off my shoulder, taking extra caution on the left side. He shakes it out, righting the inside-out arm, then drapes it over my shoulders, holding it up while I slip my arms through. He leans even closer as his hands drift around my waist, retrieving the tie on either side and tugging it around my body. For a brief moment, I'm fully encircled in his arms. We aren't exactly touching—not quite—but he's close enough for me to feel the warmth of his body, to breathe in the scent of snow and pine needles and something else spicy and sweet and uniquely *Noah.*

I expect him to hand me the ties once he's holding them both, but he keeps them until he's tied them into a neat bow just below my ribs. This is the second time he's helped me with my clothes because of my shoulder, but the first time felt clinical, a matter of expediency.

This...is not that.

Noah's gaze is heavy, the air between us thick with crackling chemistry. When his hands fall away from my body, he doesn't step away. "You don't sleep in much," he says, his voice low and husky.

I swallow against the sudden knot in my throat. "I like to use a lot of blankets."

Noah's expression isn't quite hungry, but it does feel...*admiring*. Like he's noticing me, and he likes what he sees. "You might want to rethink that for tonight," he says. "The fire will do a lot, but you might still get cold."

I resist the wildly inappropriate impulse to suggest that he stay and keep me warm and nod my head instead. "Noted. I've got sweats in my bag."

He nods like he finds my answer satisfactory and turns back toward the hallway, where he's left a bundle of firewood. "Can I bring this in?"

I smirk, pressing my lips together as I ask, "Your wood?"

He breathes out a longsuffering sigh. "I walked right into that one, didn't I?"

I grin as I take the lantern from his extended hand. "You and your *firewood* are welcome," I say.

I step out of the way, watching as he carries the bundle of wood into the room. He kneels next to the fireplace, then makes quick work of building a fire—it's clear he's done this enough that it's practically second nature.

"That should do it," he says. "It won't burn all night, but it'll help. And I can come back in the morning and build it up again."

"Thank you," I say as I move toward the fire. There's a nice sitting area next to the hearth with two swivel armchairs sitting opposite each other, a small table, and a thick, woven rug. I take the chair across from where Noah is crouched in front of the flames. "Do you think this means the reunion won't happen?"

"I doubt it," he says. "It isn't snowing hard enough for the outage to be too widespread, so I'm guessing they'll have it back on sometime tomorrow. That's what the text message from the power company said when I reported it."

"And you said it's supposed to warm up enough for the snow to melt?"

"It's hard to believe, but that's what they're saying. We should know by tomorrow afternoon what Christmas Eve will look like."

He shifts, sitting himself on the rug with his legs bent, his arms resting on his knees. His gaze drifts to the fire, and he's quiet for a long moment, but I get the sense he's working up to something, so I stay perfectly still and wait.

"Megan," he finally says, then he clears his throat. "I'm sorry about the way I..." his words trail off, and I get the sense this isn't easy for him. Not so much the apologizing, but the *talking.* "I'm sorry for the way I snapped at you earlier," he finishes. He lifts his gaze to meet mine, his eyes dark in the shadowy firelight. "I'm not great with words, and this particular subject..."

I almost step in. Reassure him. Fill the silence with my own words, which always come so easily.

But sometimes listening is just about *listening.* About letting the silence stretch as long as it needs to for words to work themselves out.

"It's tough for me," he continues. "For a lot of reasons that have to do with my dad and my own personal expectations. But you weren't wrong for asking or for offering to listen. And I was out of line for being so dismissive."

"It's totally fine," I say. "I get it."

He nods, then he reaches behind him and tugs a blanket off the arm of the other chair. He unfolds it before holding it out to me. "PICU, huh? That's a lot."

I take the blanket and drape it over my lap. "It will be, for sure. But it was my last clinical rotation in nursing school, and I loved it. I like the challenge. And kids are so much better than adults."

This makes him chuckle. "I know a lot of nurses who would disagree with you."

"My roommates disagree with me," I say. "But I love it. Give me all the kids and babies."

After another beat of silence, Noah shifts like he's going to get up. "I should let you get some sleep," he says. "Unless you need anything else?"

I could be making it up, but he almost sounds hopeful. Like he doesn't really want to leave.

"Actually, I don't really feel like sleeping yet. Do you want to stay a while? Maybe help me drink the welcome wine Olivia left for me?"

He lifts his eyebrows like he's considering, and the ensuing pause is so long, I'm positive he's going to say no. But then Noah nods. "Who can say no to welcome wine?"

Eleven

"I'm surprised you agreed to stay," I say as Noah moves to the dresser to retrieve the wine.

"Why is that?" He hands me a glass, then sets the other on the side table while he uses the corkscrew to open the bottle.

"Because it's exactly what Olivia wants," I say. "She left two wine glasses in my room, and now we're using them. I think she'd call that a win."

I hold up my glass while he fills it half full with red wine. "I won't tell her if you won't," Noah says, blue eyes sparkling in the low light. There's a smile tugging at the corners of his mouth, but he's putting up quite the fight.

It's making me itch to see it—to see a full smile and not just the tiny glimpses and snatches I've stolen so far.

He clears his throat and takes a long sip of wine. I'd put money on him doing it just to hide his face.

"What would it take?" I ask, keeping my tone light.

"What would what take?"

"What would it take to make you smile?"

"A lot of things make me smile," he says.

"Then why haven't I seen it yet?"

He rolls his eyes. "You've seen me smile."

I sit up a little taller. "I haven't. Little smirks. Tiny grins. But what would it take for you to just...let loose? To smile like there's nothing in the entire world to be sad about?"

He rubs a hand over his face, giving me the distinct impression that now he's trying *not* to smile on purpose.

"Oh, come on," I say. "I can tell you want to. You *want* to smile right now."

"I don't," he deadpans.

I scour my brain for a story—something, *anything*—that might make him crack. "My first year of nursing school, I was doing my very first head-to-toe assessment on a real patient. My instructor was present, as well as a handful of other students, so needless to say, I was *really nervous*."

I take a sip of wine, needing a tiny dose of liquid courage. Honestly, it's harder to tell this story to someone who I know has medical training, but I have a feeling winning a smile from Noah will make my own embarrassment worth it.

"So I was listening for heart sounds, growing more and more uneasy because the patient's heartbeat was so faint. I kept shifting my stethoscope, hoping to find something stronger, but on the inside, I was already rehearsing how I would tell everyone the patient was actually dying. But then my instructor reached over and moved my hand to the *other* side of the patient's chest. Where her heart *actually* was."

Noah takes a deep breath, his lips pressing together like he *wants* to smile, but he doesn't cave.

"Then there was the time I accidentally told a patient I was palpating her abdomen to check for ticklishness instead of tenderness. Or the time I set up to start an IV on the patient's right side, only to pull back the blanket and realize he didn't have a right arm."

Noah barks out a laugh, head shaking as he finally lets himself smile.

The sight is *glorious*. His entire face changes. His eyes lift, lines creasing his face in all the best ways while his lips bracket straight, white teeth.

"I need you to know that I am actually a very good nurse," I say. "At least, I will be. All of those things happened in my first semester of clinicals. Except for the IV thing. That was last month. But that could have happened to anyone."

He holds my gaze for a long moment. "I don't have any doubts about how good you'll be."

"Really?" There's a vulnerability in my tone that surprises me. I *do* think I'll be a good nurse. Assuming I can find a job. But that doesn't mean I don't still feel overwhelmed if I think too hard about nursing on my own, *without* an instructor or a preceptor watching over my shoulder. "I hope I will be."

"You'll be terrified at first," Noah says. "When you realize how much your patients are counting on you. But you get used to that. Just don't stop asking questions. If you don't know something, *ask.* Better to ask than to assume and risk screwing up."

"That's good advice," I say, then a thought pops into my head. "Wait a minute. Is this how you met my brother? As his doctor?"

Noah nods his head. "Sort of. I wasn't a doctor yet. But I did a sports medicine rotation when I was in med school and spent two weeks in Harvest Hollow shadowing the team's doctors. I met most of the players, but Alec was going through something with his knee, so I saw more of him than any of the others."

"Stupid knee," I say. "He struggled his whole career with that knee."

"He's a nice guy," Noah says, and my heart warms.

"Yeah. He's pretty great."

Noah's eyes shift back to the fire, and I take full advantage of the opportunity to study his profile, his perfectly straight nose, the scar in front of his ear that disappears into his beard.

"Do you really like it here?" I ask, and his gaze shifts to mine, his expression telling me I've surprised him with the subject change.

"It feels like home," Noah says. "But it's temporary. Another few weeks, and I'll have to figure out somewhere else to go."

"You don't want to—" I cut off my question, not wanting to push.

"It's okay," he says. "Go ahead and ask."

"I was just wondering if you would go *home* home. Are you close with your parents? I remember you mentioning they live up in Asheville."

He takes another sip of his wine. "My parents are amazing. But..." He sets down his glass and runs a hand across his beard. "It's complicated right now. My father is also a doctor. A trauma surgeon."

There's a weight to Noah's words that makes me

realize he's telling me a lot more than what his father does for a living.

"Is he upset that you're no longer practicing medicine?" I ask.

It takes Noah a long time to answer, but I'm sensing this is just how conversations are with him. That if you want him to talk, you have to be comfortable with a little bit of silence.

"He hasn't said as much," he says, "but he doesn't need to. I can see it in his eyes. He looks at me like I'm broken."

We sit for another long moment. I am in no position to offer Noah any advice, but I do want to understand. "Acknowledging my own lack of experience here," I finally say, "it isn't hard for me to imagine someone needing a break from the intensity of the ER. I don't think that makes you broken. Then again, maybe you walked away because you just didn't like what you were doing?"

This time, Noah responds almost immediately. "I love being a doctor."

I pause, wondering if he noticed the *present tense* of his words. It's different than what he said earlier, when he very distinctly told me he *wasn't* a doctor anymore.

I lean back in my chair, wrapping my arms around my knees. "Then why did you leave?"

It takes a minute, but eventually Noah begins to talk.

About a patient—an older man who was constantly in the ER due to his bad heart. He was in and out of halfway homes and shelters, but despite his many struggles, he was always affable and friendly, a lot like Noah's grandfather, so Noah took a liking to him. It was clear he needed a pacemaker, but a lack of insurance and family support created huge stumbling blocks in getting him the care he needed. Despite Noah's efforts to wade through the bureaucratic red tape required to set up the man's access to Medicare and other community-based programs, he kept falling short.

"It wasn't enough," Noah says after walking me through the challenges of the man's care. "And no one in hospital administration seemed all that concerned. He was dying, and I knew he was dying, and there was nothing I could do about it. It was just a matter of time before he collapsed from a heart attack, and I hated that everyone seemed okay with that."

"It's a frustrating system," I say. "That there's always so much bureaucracy attached to peoples' lives."

"Eventually, he did collapse from a heart attack," Noah says, his voice soft, a little distant. "At the end of a really long shift when I was already worn thin. Too many losses, not enough wins and then...there he was. Unresponsive in the trauma bay." He sniffs and rubs a hand across his face. "At that point, I'd developed some pretty destructive work habits. I lived alone, in a new city, and I hadn't made many friends." He glances up, meeting my eye like this is one part I might particularly understand, and offers me the tiniest of smirks. "It might be hard for you to believe, but I'm not the greatest at first impressions."

I chuckle and shake my head. "You're better than you think."

"At any rate, I was working too much, sleeping too little. Spending too little time doing things outside the hospital. So when I saw him in the middle of the trauma bay, I just...cracked. Yelled. Turned over an instrument tray. Demanded they keep performing CPR even after another doctor had already called time of death. I lost it."

"Which is totally understandable, considering the circumstances," I say gently.

"It isn't," Noah says, clearly unconvinced. "In the ER, you aren't supposed to lose your cool. That's why I chose it. Because that's always been one of my strengths. I don't let things get personal. But then I did. I cared too much, and I let it impact my judgment. My steadiness."

"You're human," I say. "And you're supposed to be human. And if anyone expects something different, they're wrong." I hesitate before adding, "Even your father."

"He doesn't expect..." Noah pauses and takes a breath. "It's not that. I just know I've disappointed him. And I don't know how to talk about that."

"Which is why you aren't in Italy with your family," I continue. "You're avoiding your dad?"

He lets out a little chuckle. "Perceptive."

It says something significant that Noah was so quick to defend his father. I've never met any of the Hawthornes in person, but I'm getting the sense they are incredibly family-oriented. It's hard to imagine a dad being hard on his son for reacting the way Noah did. If I had to guess, this is a problem that exists largely in Noah's own mind.

He's being harder on himself than anyone else is. That's something I recognize because I do the same thing.

"So what happened after?" I ask. "Did you quit, or..."

"Not quite," he says. "Though I did try. I was ready to walk out of the hospital and never go back, but my boss put me on leave instead. On paper, it's a six-week leave of absence on account of my mental health. But I believe my boss's exact words were to go 'find some balance and touch grass.'"

"I mean, you came to the right place then."

"Yeah. But my six weeks are almost up."

I bite my lip. "What will you do then?"

"No clue."

"But you miss it," I say. "You already said that. You miss being a doctor."

He picks up his glass and drinks the last of his wine, then leans back in his chair. "I do miss it."

"Then why not go back?"

He meets my gaze, a question clear in his expression.

"If you love it and you miss it, what's holding you back?"

"I'm holding me back," he says, a slight edge to his tone. "I'm still the same man. The same doctor. And whenever I think about going back, I'm filled with this sense of...I don't know. Dread feels like too big a word. But..."

"You're worried it will happen again?" I ask.

"It could," he says. "What do I do if it does?"

"But you already said you recognized what you were doing wrong. Working too much. Spending too much time at the hospital. If you start fresh, build some better habits, maybe talk to a therapist on a regular basis." I shift in my seat, pulling the blanket up a little higher. "Noah, you can't be the only doctor who's ever dealt with this. It isn't supposed to be easy. And you shouldn't be expected to lose your humanity so that it is."

"I can't talk to a therapist," he says, breathing out a frustrated sigh. "A therapist will make me...*talk*. I'm not...good at talking."

My heart squeezes. "You're doing okay right now."

"This is different," he says. "You're easy to talk to because you aren't filling the silence. You're giving me time to figure out what I want to say."

He says the words so casually, he can't recognize how much they impact me, but they hit me right in the gut, triggering a deep sense of longing.

I want to be the person he can talk to. The person he *chooses* to talk to.

"I can talk about the reversible causes of cardiac arrest all day long," Noah says. "But you want to talk about my feelings? I hope you aren't in a hurry because it may take a while."

"I don't think you're alone in that way," I say. "But I do think it's something that gets easier with practice. It has for me. I talk to my therapist twice a month like clockwork. And it's a lot easier now than it was at first."

He stares into the fire for a long moment before he asks, "You have a therapist?"

"Her name is Gretchen," I say. "And I wouldn't have finished nursing school without her. Or made it through my last breakup. But also, we talk when things are good too. Sometimes, I even find that more helpful. Because then she can be like, 'hey look, you see all the things you're doing to take care of yourself? Notice the patterns.'"

Noah's face is contemplative, so I wait, remembering what he said about needing time to find the right words. Eventually, he looks up and says, "I think the thing that baffles me the most is that I'm not an angry person. I don't really yell or get mad. But that day, something in me just snapped."

"Noah, you ran out of bandwidth. You were exhausted. Stressed. You can't judge yourself by your worst day."

"Yeah, maybe not. But that's easier said than done." He scrubs his hands over his face and leans back in his chair. "Man. Wow." He motions between us. "This doesn't usually happen for me."

Heat blooms and spreads through my chest. "This being...the talking?"

"The talking, the feelings. All of it." He lifts his gaze to meet mine. "It's different with you."

I offer him a teasing smile. "And here I thought I wasn't *needed* at all."

He smiles. Now that he's already done it once, they seem to be coming more easily. "I shouldn't have said that. But you have to understand my hesitation. You're probably too young for me, and the fact that Olivia—"

"Young?" I say, interrupting him. "How young do you think I am?"

"You just finished nursing school, so that makes you what, twenty-one? Twenty-two?"

"I started school late," I say. "I'm twenty-five."

"Positively ancient," he says, laughter in his tone.

There is so much we aren't saying. He's owning that Olivia might have intended to set us up, but he isn't saying whether that's good or bad. And why should he? I have no idea where I'll be working come January. And at this point, neither does he.

It's probably a terrible idea to start anything when both of our lives are so uncertain.

Then again, he just said things were different with me. And this whole conversation, I've been spending an inordinate amount of time imagining how pretty his big blue eyes would look on a baby.

Maybe we don't know what will happen next.

But I'm sure I'll regret it if I leave Stonebrook Farm without being honest about my interest—about how he makes me feel.

I drain the last of my wine, nerves spiking as I ask, "Is that why you didn't kiss me today? Outside by the tree? Because you thought I was too young for you?"

He leans forward and props his elbows on his knees. "I wanted to. I wasn't even thinking about your age.

But..." He hesitates and breathes out a sigh. "I'm a mess right now, Megan."

I reach out and grab the bottle of wine, filling my glass a second time. When I hold it up in his direction, he nods, and I fill his as well. "Well that makes two of us," I say. "I have no idea where I'm going to work next month. I have no idea if I'll pass my licensing exam or where I'm going to live or how anything is going to look in my future."

"What does that make us?" Noah asks through a chuckle.

"I have no idea," I say. "Probably perfect for each other."

He grins. "So maybe we just...finish the rest of the wine and get to know each other? See what happens?"

"I like that plan," I say. "But I do need you to tell me just one thing first."

"Anything," he says, and I can tell by the sincerity in his tone that he really means it.

"Are you *ever* going to kiss me? Because honestly, sitting here and wondering all night might actually kill me."

Fire flashes in Noah's eyes as he studies me, his gaze holding mine in that quiet way I've grown used to over the last few days. Then he shifts and stands, slowly closing the distance between us.

When he reaches me, he takes my wine glass out of my hand and sets it on the side table, then he leans down, placing his palms on either arm of my chair.

"We can't have that," he says.

My heart rate picks up speed, my skin prickling with new awareness. "No?"

He brushes his nose against mine, his breath warm on my cheek. "Nope. I like you too much for you to die over a kiss."

Finally, I think.

Then I lean up and meet his mouth with mine.

Noah's lips are fire warm and feather soft, and the contact makes heat rush through my body. The way we're positioned makes our kiss entirely PG—something my brother could see without freaking out, but somehow it still feels like...everything. Like something intangible is happening.

After several moments of gentle, tender kisses, I sit up a little taller, bringing myself closer. I want more of him. More of *this.* But I can't get close enough. I'm still sitting, and he's still standing, and *only* our lips are touching.

It's maddening.

Sensing my frustration, or maybe feeling it himself, Noah breaks the kiss long enough to stand to his full height and pull me to my feet. Wordlessly, he spins us around and sits in the chair I just vacated, then slips his hands around my waist and tugs me onto his lap so I'm facing him, my knees bracketing his hips.

"Is this okay?" he whispers as his fingers slide into my hair and press into my scalp.

"Perfect," I whisper back. Then I find his lips again.

I'm not sure I have ever believed in love at first sight. Or even love at first kiss. But I do know that I have kissed my fair share of men over the years, and no kiss has ever felt like this.

I lift my hands to Noah's cheeks and cradle his face, willing him to sense what I'm sensing, to pick up on the same intensity that's making my limbs feel molten. This kiss is rewiring my body, rewriting my programming to be tuned in to him like I've never been tuned in to anyone before.

When I deepen the kiss, my tongue brushing against his bottom lip, Noah lets out a low groan that makes my blood run even hotter. This man is impossibly attractive, sexy in ways that make it very easy to imagine forgetting everything but the feel of his body under my hands.

But something else is happening here. Something bigger.

Somehow, I know with utter certainty.

This kiss—this moment—it's a beginning for both of us.

When our lips finally part, I'm almost afraid to meet Noah's eye. But then he brushes a kiss to my forehead and utters a simple, "Wow."

I chuckle into his chest, wrapping my arms around him while his hands settle against my back. "Yeah, that about sums it up."

After I begrudgingly let Noah get up long enough to put another log on the fire, we settle back into the same chair and talk for hours.

We touch on almost everything. The big things—politics, religion, world views. But we also talk about food and pets and vacations. We list our favorite books and our favorite movies and talk about how we like to spend our free time. We discover we both love hiking, though I'd rather die than sleep on the ground, and he's an avid backpacker, happy to stay on the trail for days.

I tell him about Juno and how much I loved watching my best friend become a mom. He tells me about his three younger brothers. About being the oldest in a family of boys. He talks about med school and his decision to practice emergency medicine. How he feels like the ER is the one place where decisions and words come to him easily.

Except, the words are also coming easily *now*. No long pauses, no more hesitation. I'm not sure he's noticed, but *I'm* noticing, and it's really making my heart happy.

"You're getting sleepy," Noah says after a particularly long lull in the conversation. It isn't a bad lull. Not awkward at all. But he's right. I *am* getting sleepy.

I drop my head onto his shoulder and close my eyes. "Yeah. But I don't want to go to bed. You're good company."

"Come on," he says, giving my hip a good-natured squeeze. "Sleep. We have all day tomorrow."

I grumble as I shift and stand, but I also let out an enormous yawn, so I can't truly argue.

Once he's on his feet, Noah picks up the blanket that fell on the floor and wraps it around my shoulders, pulling it closed just under my chin.

"Stay warm tonight," he says, the firelight flickering across his face.

I push up on my toes and press my lips against his. "I will because of you."

He lingers, kissing me one more time, then he steps away and moves toward the door. The absence of his warmth triggers a sudden and intense longing, and a tiny sense of panic wells up in my chest. Like him leaving might end whatever magic we've felt tonight.

"Noah," I say just as he reaches the door. He turns,

one hand on the doorknob, and looks at me over his shoulder.

I lick my lips. "What are you thinking right now?"

I'm not sure what sort of answer I'm looking for. Maybe just confirmation that he's feeling this too.

Noah's voice floats across the darkness, wrapping around me like an embrace. "I'm thinking that maybe my family knows what's best for me after all."

Twelve

THE POWER IS ON BY THE TIME I WAKE UP THE NEXT morning. When I walk to the window and look outside, the sky is a brilliant blue, the sun sparkling as it reflects off the newly fallen snow. For a split second, I wonder if last night was some sort of glorious fever dream. But the burned-down embers of the fire Noah built are right there in the hearth. He was here. *We kissed.*

And it was incredible.

I lift a hand to my lips, the memory of his touch still fresh enough to start a low fire in my belly. I need to call Evie. Tell her what happened. But I'm guessing Noah is already up, which means I'd rather get downstairs as quickly as possible.

As amazing as last night was, it's hard not to sense

the looming countdown clock ticking down the moments to when I'm supposed to leave.

I take a quick shower and get dressed, careful of my still tender shoulder, then head downstairs where I find Noah in the kitchen, warm coffee waiting and a stack of waffles on the counter.

Noah is wearing an apron, his shirt sleeves rolled up to his elbows, and he's wearing glasses, something I haven't seen on him until right now. He smiles when he sees me step into the kitchen, and he looks utterly and completely adorable. It's hard to believe the scowly man who rescued me at the beginning of the week is the same guy.

"Good morning," he says. He motions toward my shoulder with the spatula he's holding. "How's it feeling?"

"A little sore," I say. "But still functional."

I stand awkwardly in the doorway, not sure how to behave in this new normal. I feel an impulse to walk over and wrap my arms around Noah, kiss him hello, but...is that what he wants too? Is that something you do the morning after a first kiss?

"I never did get you a sling," Noah says. "I can if you think you need one."

"I think I'm okay. I'm trying to be careful."

He eyes me, like his doctor brain is dubious that I'll

be as careful as I should be, but he must decide not to press the point because he lets the topic go. He gestures to the waffles. "I don't suppose you want a waffle? Or four?"

I slip onto a barstool across from him. "I'd love *a* waffle. Not sure about four."

"I probably should have halved the recipe. But I didn't really think about it until I'd already started. My mom says I can freeze these though."

My heart squeezes the tiniest bit. "You called your mom about waffles? In Italy?"

"She's only six hours ahead," he says with an easy shrug. "It was good to talk to her."

There is a lightness about Noah that feels new. He's relaxed, his words coming as easily as they did last night. I can't help but hope the change has something to do with me, at least in small part. But more than that, I hope that talking things out helped him process a little of how he's feeling.

Noah slides a waffle onto my plate, then moves the butter dish and a ceramic syrup jar close enough for me to reach. "Want coffee?"

I nod, and he makes quick work of pouring me a mug, following my milk and sugar instructions until it's in my hands, warm and perfectly delicious.

"When did the power turn back on?" I ask.

"Around six," he says. "The high is close to fifty today, so most of the snow will probably melt by tomorrow."

I take a long sip of my coffee, keenly aware that after the most intense makeout of my life, Noah and I are sitting here talking about the weather like there's nothing else to say. But everything I *want* to say feels big. Monumental.

Can I really look at him over morning coffee and just casually drop that after last night, I'm pretty sure he's ruined kissing for every other man on the planet? It's him or no one. I can't go back.

"I should check in with the Petersons and make sure they're still good to come," I say.

Noah nods. "I'll get the farm road cleared today, and I expect the county will get the highway plowed. If the Petersons need any reassurance, tell them I really do think the roads will be fine."

"Good. Perfect." My hand is trembling as I pick up my fork, which is completely ridiculous. But Noah in glasses, feeding me, making me coffee. It's too much for my heart. I can hardly breathe for the weight of my longing. I want this—*him*—like I've never wanted anything before.

I take a steadying breath, but when I try to cut my waffle, my hand slips, and a syrup-covered chunk goes flying across the counter and lands next to Noah's plate. My face flushes hot as he grins, giving me a sideways glance. "You okay over there?"

I clear my throat. "Totally fine."

I spear the runaway waffle and pop it into my mouth. But when I go to cut a second bite, I drop the knife and it bumps against the table, then clatters onto the floor.

I close my eyes as Noah starts to chuckle.

"Don't laugh at me," I say as I lift my hands to cover my face, but I can't blame him. I'm laughing at myself. "I don't know what's wrong with me."

He stands and reaches for my knife, his free hand grazing across my shoulders as he moves into the kitchen and drops the offending utensil into the sink. He grabs a clean one from the drawer and slides it across the counter to me before returning to his seat.

"Thank you." I take the knife and set it next to my plate. "I think I'm just nervous."

"Why?" he asks, and I look over at him. His expression is open and warm, making it easy to respond.

"Because I like you so much."

He holds my gaze for a long moment. "You shouldn't be nervous."

"No? Why not?"

He grins, then leans forward and presses a lingering

kiss to my lips. He tastes like coffee and maple syrup. "Because I like you so much," he says.

The kiss goes a long way to ease my nerves, and I manage to make it through the rest of breakfast without dropping anything else. By the time we're done doing the dishes, I'm feeling pretty good.

Tomorrow is Christmas Eve.

For now, I'm just going to enjoy the holiday. Enjoy *Noah.*

And we *do* enjoy it.

Well, first we both have to do a little bit of work. While he plows the main farm road—a tractor with a snowplow attachment makes it relatively easy work—I read through Olivia's final checklist of Peterson family reunion preparations.

After I call the Petersons to make sure the weather hasn't disrupted their plans, I check in with the catering staff and give them a final headcount. Then I rearrange the tables in the dining room and put together Christmas centerpieces for each one.

Since several of the Peterson grandchildren are bringing significant others to the reunion, the Peterson grandmother has made a particular request that mistletoe hang from every door frame. There's a big box of fake mistletoe in the storage closet, so I tie together several bunches, then scoot a chair into the closest doorway.

With the largest bunch in one hand and a thumbtack in the other, I climb onto the chair and reach up, hesitating when a dull ache radiates through my shoulder. I drop my arms again—Noah will have to do this for me—but then the front door opens, and the man himself steps inside.

His eyes widen when he sees me on the chair. "Seriously?" he says as he strides toward me.

"What?" I say. "I need to hang the mistletoe."

"You *need* to stay on the ground where you can't hurt yourself again." He moves his hands to my waist and gently lifts me, lowering me down. I don't mind that even when I'm safely on the floor, he keeps his hands on me, his fingers encircling my waist.

"You're right," I say. "I realized as much when I tried to reach over my head." I lift the mistletoe. "Hang it for me?"

He leans down and kisses me. "You shouldn't be lifting your arms, but I'm more concerned you were standing on a chair. With the tenderness in your shoulder, you're more susceptible to repeat injury." He gives my hips a little squeeze. "Please. Stay on the ground for me."

His concern is both endearing and adorable.

"Fine," I say. "But that means you can't leave again. I have six of these I need to hang up."

He tugs me closer, one hand wrapping around my back while the other takes the mistletoe out of my hand. "Does that mean I get to kiss you under all six?"

I grin. "You don't need mistletoe to kiss me."

"Good thing," he says. Then his mouth takes mine one more time.

LATE THE FOLLOWING AFTERNOON, the Petersons arrive at Stonebrook in a caravan of minivans and SUVs. Catering staff have been in and out all day, hauling food from the catering kitchen down by the restaurant up to the farmhouse. The food smells delicious, Christmas carols are playing through the house, and I've got to say, the decorations really do look on point.

Several of the Petersons mention the gorgeous Christmas tree as they walk into the main room, and I make a mental note to relay their praise to Noah.

He's out at the goat barn now, making the rounds, tending to the animals like he does every night, but I'm guessing he'll linger a little longer tonight, if only to avoid the crowd.

As far as I can tell, there are four generations of

Petersons at the party, from the oldest who has to be in her nineties, all the way down to the youngest who is just shy of three months old.

They are a gregarious group, boisterous and happy and clearly thrilled to be together.

After welcoming them all and giving them a quick rundown of how their evening will go—cocktails and appetizers, then dinner and dessert whenever they're ready—I sneak into the kitchen to fix myself a small plate from the tray of extras the catering staff set out for Noah and me.

Noah surprises me, stepping up behind me and slipping his hands around my waist. "Hi," he whispers, voice close to my ear. "You look beautiful."

I lean into him, loving the feel of his warm chest at my back. "Do I?" I've changed clothes since he last saw me, putting on a red wrap dress that Evie made me buy the last time we went shopping together because, according to her, it complements my wavy brown hair and makes my boobs look amazing.

"You do," Noah says. "You smell good too."

I turn in his arms so I can face him. "I'm surprised to see you back inside. I thought you might camp out with the goats tonight."

"I was tempted," he says, "but I was also hungry." He reaches over my shoulder and plucks a stuffed mushroom off the tray, then pops it into his mouth. His eyes close as he chews and he lets out a little moan that makes my blood heat.

New favorite activity: watching Noah Hawthorne enjoy his food.

"If you ever have the chance, you should really come back when the restaurant's open," he says as he reaches for another mushroom. "It's the best food I've ever eaten, and I'm not just saying that because Lennox is family."

"Lennox is the chef?"

Noah nods.

"An award-winning chef and a famous movie star in the same family feels very glamorous."

"Honestly, they're all ridiculously talented," Noah says. "Which would be annoying if they weren't also ridiculously likable."

"What about your brothers?" I help myself to a cracker topped with baked brie and sour cherry jam. "I feel like we talked about your childhood, but I don't think you've mentioned what they're doing now."

Behind us, the kitchen is bustling with activity, with caterers coming in and out, refreshing appetizer trays or working on dinner prep. But in this corner, over by the espresso machine, Noah and I are mostly out of the way.

I wouldn't say we have enough privacy for any real

conversation, but for something this casual, I'm happy to ignore the fact that we aren't as alone as we were last night.

"My brothers," Noah says, like the subject brings him some level of amusement. "They're great guys. Smart and talented. But sometimes I feel like we're living on different planets."

"In what way?"

"Let's see. Mason has an MBA, and he's always made tons of money, even though I don't think he's ever liked any of the jobs he's had. Then there's Spencer. He went to law school but never took the bar, deciding instead to open a consulting firm. He's very strategic and he's great with people, so he's all about maximizing performance and creating good company culture. But he started his company with zero experience. He just decided he was going to do it, and then he did."

"Sounds brave?" I say.

"*Now* it seems brave because it worked," Noah says. "But when he first started, it just seemed reckless. But all three of them are like that. They just *do stuff*."

"I know people like that," I say. "I get what you're saying. What about the third one?"

Noah lets out a little chuckle. "That's Will. He went to one semester of college, then dropped out and moved to Europe where he hitchhiked across France, working odd jobs and learning everything he possibly could about wine. He came home six months ago and convinced Mason and Spencer to buy a winery with him."

"Oh wow. That feels big."

Noah scans the tray behind me. "Your face is saying you just took a bite of something really good."

"Amazing," I say, pointing to the brie-topped crackers. "Right there. Try one of those."

Noah picks one up, then grabs another and hands it to me. "I guess it could be big?" he says, going back to the conversation about his brothers. "I'm not sure I really understand everything they're doing. There's an old hotel and a restaurant on the property, but that whole part of it is totally rundown. Hasn't been operable in years, so they've got their work cut out for them. They convinced Flint to go in on it with them. That's how they could afford to buy it in the first place."

It's interesting hearing Noah talk about his brothers. His expression is very stern, and though his tone isn't *quite* judgmental, he definitely has an *older brother* vibe that I haven't heard before.

"What?" Noah says, clearly reading my expression. "Why are you looking at me like that?"

I grin. "Tell me you're the oldest, most responsible

brother without telling me you're the oldest, most responsible brother."

Noah gives me a sheepish grin. "I'm probably too hard on them."

"I totally get it," I say. "My brother is super protective of me. Annoyingly so sometimes."

Noah's eyebrows lift. "Should I be concerned about that?"

The question sends a thrill racing through me. Because it speaks of a future we haven't talked about yet —a future I wasn't sure Noah was going to want.

He must realize the same thing because he quickly backpedals. "Not that I'm saying we're—or that we're not. But if we were—if that's something you wanted, then maybe—"

I lift a hand to his chest. "Hey," I say, patting him gently. His pectoral muscle twitches under my hand, and for a split second, I wonder what Noah might look like shirtless. He's broad-shouldered, with a trim waist, but I've only ever seen him in multiple layers, so there's a lot left to the imagination. Still, this is not the time or place to give in to that particular distraction, so I force myself to meet his gaze.

There's a question there, and a healthy dose of trepidation, like he's bracing himself for bad news. "Whatever you're thinking, I want it," I say. "I have no idea how or where or even when, but I'd like to try."

He smiles, then picks up my hand, lifting it to his lips to press a kiss against the pad of my thumb. "Then I guess you should probably give me your number."

I step a little closer, and he pulls me against him, wrapping his arms around my waist. "That is a very good idea."

From the other room, a loud chorus of laughter erupts followed by cheers and applause.

I tilt my head in the direction of the noise. "I should probably go check on everyone. See if they're ready for dinner."

He nuzzles his nose into my hair. "Do you have to?" His lips are close enough that I feel their movement against my skin, and the sensation sends a cascade of gooseflesh down my arms.

"It's why I'm here," I say. "But you're welcome to come with me."

Noah leans back and grimaces, and I immediately start to laugh.

"Fine, forget I asked," I say. "Go hide in your room while I host the party." There's something endearing about his reluctance to stay if only because it's so completely *Noah*. And now I know him enough to realize as much.

"I'll stay with you if you want me to," Noah quickly says. "I promise I will."

I lean up on my toes and press a quick kiss to his lips. "My words might have sounded teasing, but I meant them. I'll be fine. Just a reminder, though: if Olivia hadn't hired me for the week, it would probably be *you* hosting this party."

"My cousin is brilliant," he says. "Smartest woman on the planet. Well, second to you."

"That was the right answer, Noah Hawthorne," I say, then I let him pull me in for one last kiss.

Thirteen

THE REUNION IS BUSTLING AND HAPPY, AND THERE ISN'T much for me to do other than stand back and make sure everyone is having a good time. Especially once they start dinner.

But there's one member of the family who keeps catching my eye—a little girl, maybe ten or eleven, who really doesn't look like she feels well. Halfway through dinner, her dad walks her over to a couch in the living room and helps her stretch out, propping a pillow under her head.

I grab a blanket off a nearby chair and walk over. "Everything okay?"

"Thank you," the dad says as he takes the blanket and drapes it over his daughter. "She's just got a tummy ache. Is it okay if she rests here for a bit?"

"Of course. I can keep an eye on her." I look down at the little girl. "Do you want some water? Maybe some ginger ale?"

She gives her head a shallow shake. "I don't want anything."

"Hey, Joe," someone calls from the dining room. "Come tell the story about you and Bree in Chicago."

Joe looks toward the table, then looks back at me, uncertainty marring his expression.

"I really don't mind watching her," I say. "I'm a nurse. So this is totally in my comfort zone." I can only hope Joe didn't catch the tiny hitch in my voice as I said the words. I've been *almost* a nurse for so long, it still feels weird to drop the almost and just claim the job title.

"Oh, wow. That's great then." He crouches down in front of his daughter. "I won't be far, okay? If you need me, I'll be here in seconds."

As soon as Joe is back in the dining room, I take up the spot he just left, crouching in front of the little girl. "What's your name, sweetie?" I ask as I brush her hair off her face.

She licks dry lips, her eyelids fluttering closed. "Sabrina," she says softly.

"Hi, Sabrina. My name's Megan."

She's warm enough that I wish I had a thermometer

to take her temperature. She definitely feels like she has a fever.

"Can you tell me what hurts?"

She winces, drawing her knees up to her belly. "My tummy," she says.

"Do you think you ate something that didn't sit right? Maybe too many Christmas cookies?"

She shakes her head no. "I haven't eaten anything." She frowns, her forehead creasing as she lets out a little whimper. "Ow, ow, ow."

Suspicion nags at my brain as I look at her curled up form, at the tension in the set of her shoulders. "Sabrina, how long has your tummy hurt? Do you know? Did it hurt before you came to the party?"

"A little," she says. "Mommy said I might just be hungry."

"Does it hurt worse now than it did before?"

Sabrina nods.

I move closer and sit on the coffee table, debating my next steps.

It's probably nothing. When kids have a stomachache, it usually *is* nothing.

But Sabrina's pain seems severe. With the fever and her lack of appetite, it could be something more serious. Appendicitis, maybe. And if that's what it is, Sabrina needs to get to the hospital as quickly as possible.

I reach out and put a tentative hand on her knee. "Hey, do you think you can lower your legs for me? Just long enough to point out where you're hurting."

At first, Sabrina shakes her head.

"If we're really quick?" I say.

Slowly, she lowers her legs, letting out another whimper as she does. I move my hand to the lower right quadrant of her abdomen and lightly press against the outside of her party dress. "Right here?"

She nods, then cries, "I want my dad."

I pull the blanket back over her. "Let me get him for you, okay?"

I hurry to the dining room and motion for Joe to get back to his daughter, then I make a beeline for Noah's room.

I'm pretty sure it's appendicitis. But I'm not technically a nurse yet—not until I pass my licensing exam. Can I really be sure enough to break up a reunion and send a family down the mountain to the hospital in Silver Creek?

Maybe—if I were the only one here.

But I'm not. And I'm guessing Noah has diagnosed appendicitis a lot more times than I have.

I knock on his door, heart hammering.

"Noah?" I call, knocking again when he doesn't answer, this time with a little more urgency.

Finally, the door swings open. And *oh. Oh my.* It's like my earlier imaginings conjured him because Noah is standing in front of me very, *very* shirtless. Sweatpants sitting low on his hips. Bare chest. Shower damp hair. And the tattoo on his forearm—I can see the whole thing now since there's no shirt to block my view. It's a tree, branches and leaves growing up his arm and wrapping around his bicep.

I have never been so disappointed that my ethical and moral duty requires me to ignore the glorious sight of Noah's torso and focus on the crisis at hand.

"Hi," I manage to say, my voice a little too breathless. "Are you busy?"

"Not at all. Is everything okay?" He still has a towel in his hand, and he uses it to reach up and dry off his hair.

"I don't think so, actually. I'm pretty sure there's a little girl on the living room couch who has appendicitis."

He frowns, tossing his towel onto the bed. "How sure is pretty sure?" He turns and walks to his dresser where he riffles through a drawer and pulls out a t-shirt, tugging it over his head.

"She has a fever. Hasn't eaten anything since she got here but has intense pain on the lower right side of her abdomen. I know I could just send them to the hospital, but I'm pretty sure that would end the party, so I wanted to see if you would examine her first. Just to make sure."

He nods. "It's fine. You were right to come get me." He quickly retrieves a duffel bag from under his bed and pulls out a stethoscope, filling me with an immediate sense of relief that he's willing to help. "Let's go," he says, and then we're off.

When we make it back to the living room, Joe has Sabrina in his lap, and a woman I assume is his wife has joined him, the worry on her face a mirror of her husband's.

"She's not okay, is she?" Joe asks as I approach.

Instead of answering, I step to the side and motion to Noah. "Joe, this is my friend, Noah, and he's a doctor. I think you should let him take a look at Sabrina, okay?"

Joe quickly agrees, and Noah makes quick work of examining the little girl. Most of the family has abandoned the dining room, instead hovering around the edges of the room as they watch Noah work.

Just like yesterday when he was taking care of me, his movements are quick and sure, his voice steady. He explains to Sabrina and her dad exactly what he's doing as he palpates her abdomen, then uses his stethoscope to listen for bowel sounds. I'll never claim that I don't appreciate toned abdominal muscles or defined biceps. It's nice that Noah has those. But I would argue that at the end of the day, I'm most attracted to competence. To skill. Seeing Noah do something he has trained years to do is incredibly sexy.

When he finishes his exam, he glances at me and nods.

It feels good to be right, but I hate what this means for Sabrina. Because she's going to wake up on Christmas morning in a hospital bed.

Noah helps Sabrina into her dad's arms, then walks with them to the front door. At this point, they can drive down to the hospital faster than an ambulance could make it here, then make the same journey back down the mountain, but Noah promises to call ahead and make sure the hospital is ready for them.

In a matter of minutes, the rest of the Petersons are all preparing to go, gathering coats and bags and the Christmas presents they exchanged before dinner. I can't truly blame them. It would feel strange to keep the party going, but as I overhear everyone talking, it sounds more like they're simply relocating—taking the party to the hospital so they can all stay abreast of Sabrina's well-being.

As soon as I hear this is the plan, I help the catering staff pack up the triple chocolate cheesecake the family was supposed to have for dessert.

I'm in the kitchen, elbow deep in to-go containers,

when I see Noah step out of his room, his boots and coat on, and move toward the back door. I frown as I take in the sight of him. Something seems off. There's tension in his shoulders and through his jaw, and his brow is furrowed.

"Noah," I call, but he doesn't stop or even glance in my direction. I watch as he opens the door and disappears into the darkness, closing it behind him with a resounding *thud*.

The kitchen is noisy, so it's possible he just didn't hear me call out to him.

Then again, it's not lost on me that Noah came to Stonebrook Farm to get *away* from practicing medicine, and now, two days in a row, he's been asked to do just that. He didn't hesitate to help Sabrina—he wouldn't. Just like he didn't hesitate to help me. But during our conversation last night, I didn't get the impression that Noah has done much processing. With the end of his six weeks looming, and now, back-to-back evenings where he's been required to be the doctor he isn't sure he wants to be—it would make sense if he's upset. Or at least feeling really overwhelmed.

"Okay, that's the last of it," Kendra says. Stonebrook's catering manager has been standing beside me, slicing cheesecake, then shifting it over to me to place in individually portioned containers. But that was the last slice, which means we're done. She takes the remaining containers and adds them to a bag at her feet.

"Perfect. Thank you," I say. "I'll walk these out front."

"Take these too," Kendra says, retrieving a covered tray of Christmas cookies. "Tell them we put plastic silverware in the bag."

It takes another ten minutes to get the last of the Petersons out the door. There are missing coats and a missing wallet and a little boy who somehow managed to lose only one of his socks.

Through every eternally long moment, all I can think about is Noah. Is he okay? Is he upset? Does he need me?

Finally, *finally,* we get everyone sorted, and I send them out the door with cheesecake, cookies, and the most cheerful Merry Christmas I can manage.

It sounded a little deflated, if I'm being honest, but I doubt anyone else noticed.

Once the farmhouse door is closed behind the Petersons, my first impulse is to race upstairs and change my shoes so I can go after Noah. But now that I have the actual opportunity to do so, I'm not sure it's the right call.

If he left, he must have felt a need for some alone time. I want Noah to *want* to talk to me, but I don't want to force him if he isn't ready. He made a point of mentioning that he appreciates the way I don't fill the silence and give him time to find his words.

So maybe I need to do the same thing now.

I head into the kitchen to see if there's anything I can do to help clean up, but Kendra quickly walks me right back out the door. "You already did your part," she says. "We've got this. Go relax."

I won't truly relax until Noah's back and I can ask him if he's okay.

So what do I do instead?

"Hey, you haven't happened to see Noah come inside, have you?" I ask Kendra.

She shakes her head no. "I didn't even notice he left. Is everything okay? You two looked pretty cozy earlier."

"Things are good," I say a little too quickly, but I hardly sound convincing.

Kendra studies me for a moment, then walks to the fridge. She opens it and pulls out half of a triple chocolate cheesecake. "Here. You look like you need this."

"I didn't think there was any left."

She shrugs. "I saved a little for you and Noah." She reaches into the drawer behind her and pulls out a fork, then hands it over. "But I won't tell him if you don't save him any."

"Thank you," I say. "Seriously, you're an absolute lifesaver."

I carry the cheesecake into the living room, not even bothering to get myself a plate. Tonight feels like an eat-right-of-the-pan kind of night.

The fire has burned down a little, so I add a couple more pieces of wood, then settle onto the couch and try not to think about Noah while I eat my weight in cheesecake.

The sugar is an excellent distraction, but the longer Noah is gone, the more I start to worry. It's not like we had plans. But after how good things seemed earlier, I expected that after the Petersons left, we'd spend the rest of the evening together.

Then again, it's not hard to understand why Noah might need time to think. He's in the middle of something big—something that doesn't have anything to do with me. I can't just expect him to be fine because I'm here and I'd really like to spend my Christmas Eve with him.

I sigh and help myself to another bite.

Thirty minutes later, I've eaten half of what was left in the pan, and my worries have spiraled from perfectly logical and grounded in reason to slightly unhinged with a touch of delusional.

My brain does not hold back. I worry about everything from Noah freezing to death or getting mauled by a bear to him deciding I'm a terrible kisser and he'd rather spend the evening with the goats than face me and tell me the truth.

I'm not so out of control that I can't fight the ridiculous with logic. It's forty-seven degrees outside, and Noah grew up in these mountains. He's not going to freeze. And while I don't have concrete evidence that my kissing is fine, I feel like, at twenty-five, someone would have told me by now if I were really bad at it.

But that's the thing about worry. The longer you spiral, the less realistic it becomes.

I toss my fork into the almost empty pan and groan as I drop back onto the couch cushions. "Gah, Megan!" I say to myself. "Get a grip!"

I stare at the ceiling for a long moment, then roll over to face the fire. If it wasn't Christmas Eve, I'd call Alec and Evie. But we already talked once this morning, and I don't want to interrupt their evening.

So I guess I'm on my own.

Just me and my cheesecake.

I look at the fork I left balanced on the edge of the pan and debate whether it's worth reaching for one more bite. I stretch my arm out, my fingers barely grazing the edge of the utensil, and it flips out of my reach and tumbles to the floor.

You know what? That's probably better. Eating my feelings can only get me so far.

I reach up and tug at the blanket draped over the back of the sofa, then spread it over me. Before long, my thoughts finally settle, and I start to feel sleepy. It's only just past nine, but I'm on a comfortable couch, staring into a soothing fire, and I just ate myself into a sugar coma. As soon as I let my eyelids fall closed, I drift off.

It's Noah who wakes me up, his cool hand cupping my cheek.

"Hey," he says softly when my eyes flutter open. "Sorry to wake you."

It takes me a moment to process my surroundings, his presence beside me. He looks chilled, his nose a little pink like he's been outside. But his face is relaxed, his expression open.

"I thought you might want to go upstairs," he says. "You'll be more comfortable in your bed than you are here."

"What time is it?"

"Just after eleven."

"I don't want to go upstairs," I say as the last fog of sleep clears from my mind. "I was waiting for you."

I shift and sit up, and Noah moves from where he's crouching in front of the couch so he can sit next to me.

"I'm sorry I disappeared," he says. "I just needed some time to think."

"I figured," I say. "But I was worried about you." I look over at the cheesecake. "I ate a lot of my feelings."

Noah lets out a little chuckle. "I'm sorry I missed it. But I'm most sorry I made you worry."

He leans back into the cushions, then tugs me closer. I settle in next to him, my head on his chest and his arm wrapped around me.

"Where did you go?" I ask.

"All over," Noah says. "Just walking. Thinking."

"I almost came looking for you," I say. "But I wasn't sure if you would want me to. And also I thought I might get lost."

He leans down and presses a kiss to the side of my head. "I appreciate you giving me some space." He's quiet for a beat before he adds, "I dated a woman while I was in med school who didn't know how to do that. The longer we were together, the more she made me feel like I was—I don't know. Basically just *wrong* all the time. We would have these conversations, and she would want me to talk about my feelings immediately. On her timeline. I didn't get time to think or even breathe. She wanted answers. Commitments. Feelings. On demand. All the time."

"Sounds intense," I say. It's the first time he's ever mentioned a past relationship, and I'm surprised by the flare of jealousy the subject triggers. Apparently, my heart already believes Noah is mine.

"I recognize, in hindsight, that there's definitely stuff I can work on," he says. "I probably *should* talk to a therapist. Get better at opening up. But I also think we're all built differently. And she could have given me more room to figure myself out."

"She could have," I agree. "It's not wrong to need a little time to sort how you feel."

"Here's the thing though," Noah says. "Had you come outside to find me, I would have welcomed your company. I wanted it, even. It's a full moon and the night sky is beautiful, and I just kept thinking, 'I wish Megan were here to see this with me.'"

I lean back, sitting up enough for me to see Noah's face.

"It's different with you," he says. "A week of us knowing each other, and I already know it's different. How is that possible?"

I lift a hand to his cheek, then lean in and press my lips to his. "I don't know," I say. "But I feel the same way."

I still have so many questions. But with Noah sitting beside me, it's easy to trust that whatever the answers are, it's going to be okay. If Noah doesn't want to practice medicine anymore, he'll find something else to do. I don't care what it is just so long as he's happy. Which makes it easy to let go of needing an answer right this moment. It's not a choice that's about me anyway, so he'll tell me when he's ready.

We kiss until my mind grows hazy with desire, my blood running several degrees hotter than normal. But then Noah pulls back.

"Wait, wait." He grips my arms and presses his forehead to mine. "I have to tell you something, and I'm going to lose my focus if we keep this up."

I grin and bite my lip. There's something intoxicating about the slight rasp in Noah's voice, the realization that he's this undone because of me. But I really *do* want to hear what he has to say, so I force myself to sit back, putting a healthy measure of space between us.

"Okay. I'm ready."

He looks at me like it's taking all of his resolve to keep his distance, then he lets out a little growl and leans in to kiss me one more time. "Stop looking at me like that," he says through a chuckle, his lips close to mine. "You have to stop smiling. I can't resist you when you're smiling."

"Then stop making me smile," I say, but I'm already kissing him again, so I'm not sure I really mean it.

Another few moments pass before I pull back. "Okay, for real," I say. "Words. Sentences. We can do this." This time, I stand and move to an armchair sitting perpendicular to the couch. "This will make it easier."

"Good thinking," Noah says. He takes a deep breath, then shifts and leans forward, propping his elbows on his knees. "So, when we were talking the other night, I didn't mention that the hospital where I've been working the last couple of years is Northvale General."

My eyebrows lift. "You live in Charlotte? But that's—that's my program. That's where I want to work."

So many thoughts run through my mind.

First and foremost: if I get a spot in the PICU nurse residency and Noah goes back to work, we'll be working in the same hospital. Living in the same town. It's almost too good to be true.

He nods. "The other thing I haven't told you is I happen to know the nursing coordinator on the peds floor. She's in charge of hiring, and I took the liberty of sending her an email." His expression turns a little sheepish. "About you."

My heart starts pounding. "You did?"

"I was very professional," Noah says. "I just told her you come highly recommended by your program, and I know you personally and can vouch for your credibility as a person and as a nurse. It was only in the postscript that I told her how much I'd really like to be able to make out with you in the on-call room."

I suck in a gasp "You did not."

He grins. "You're right. I did not. And I really *don't* know if my email will matter."

"But you tried," I say, suddenly feeling emotional. "It means a lot to me that you tried."

Only then does it occur to me that making out with me in the on-call room would mean...

"Noah, are you going back to work?"

His expression shifts, his gaze dropping to the floor for a long moment. But then he looks up, eyes clear as he says, "I've been talking to someone really smart lately. And she made me realize it's okay to be human. To make mistakes." He takes a deep breath. "I have to do things differently. Find a better balance. And I meant what I said about talking to a therapist. But yeah. I want to go back."

I dart off the chair and I'm back in his arms in a second, pulling him into the world's biggest hug. Even when I pull away, he keeps me close, his fingers threaded through mine. "If you don't get a spot in the PICU, I very selfishly want you to know there are other units at Northvale that are really great. And other hospitals in Charlotte. I'd love for you to be close."

He squeezes my hands, and I close my eyes, needing a moment to think, to regroup, to assess the *very big* feelings running through me.

Had someone asked me a week ago if I would ever move to a different city for a man, I would have laughed. But everything about this week has been larger than life. Our conversations, our kisses. It hasn't been normal.

Maybe it's the holiday or the snow or the isolation, but I feel like I've gotten to know him better in the past few days than I usually do through months of dating someone. I know without having to even think about it. For Noah, I'd move to Charlotte tomorrow. With or without a job.

It's a completely irrational thought, and yet, it feels like the only possible choice.

I want to be with him.

And *fine*. I would also like to have a job.

But he's right. There are several hospitals in Charlotte. I could find work. I could find work and we could be together.

"I love that you're going back. And we'll work on balance together. I'll need it too since wherever I end up working, it's going to be all new for me. But can I make one more suggestion?"

Noah nods. "Of course."

"I think you should talk to your dad, Noah. I really think he'll understand."

He takes a long, slow breath, then he lets out a little

chuckle. "It sounds so easy when you say it. Makes me wonder why I've had such a hard time."

"Everything is bigger inside our heads," I say. "I think sometimes just saying our feelings out loud makes it easier to process and understand them."

He holds my gaze for a long moment. "Will you really move to Charlotte?"

"If I can find a job, yeah. It's where I wanted to end up anyway. You're just a bonus."

He grins, then pulls me in for another kiss.

"Our families are going to think we've lost our minds," I say against his mouth.

He chuckles. "I don't know. I think Olivia might be pretty happy."

"So you're giving her the win, then?" I ask. "Officially?"

"If she needs it," he says like it's no big deal. Then he pulls me into a long, lingering kiss before saying, "But I'm the one who's really won."

I try to think of a response, something worthy of the sentiment, but then Noah shifts, moving his mouth to my neck and the attention he gives the skin just below my earlobe robs me of all rational thought. So I surrender. I let the rest of my words go, and I fall into his kisses, get lost in his touch.

We stay there on the couch, wrapped up in each

other's arms long enough that at some point, we both decide we can't be bothered to split up and head to our own rooms. The couch is comfortable enough, and there's something magical about falling asleep in the soft glow of the flickering fire and the twinkle lights on the tree.

I lift my head from where it's resting on Noah's chest and prop my chin up so I can look at him. His face is relaxed, his eyes closed. "You are a very good Christmas present, Noah Hawthorne."

He grins. "You aren't so bad yourself. The best Christmas present I had no idea I wanted."

"Thank goodness for Olivia," I say as I tuck myself back into his shoulder.

He leans forward and presses a kiss to the top of my head. "Thank goodness for Olivia."

Fourteen

IT FEELS FITTING THAT, SINCE HER NAME WAS THE LAST thing we uttered before falling asleep on the couch, Olivia is the first thing I see when I wake up the next morning.

At least, I *think* it's Olivia. Based on Noah's very groggy, "Olivia?" just seconds after we're both jostled awake, it feels like a reasonable assumption.

The woman looming over us has stunning red hair and wide green eyes and a smile bright enough for a toothpaste commercial. Her eyes keep darting back from me, to Noah, then back to me again.

I can't be sure, because I have only been awake for a matter of moments, but she appears *very* happy to have found us asleep on the couch together.

"What are you doing here?" Noah says as we both shift and sit up.

"We came home," Olivia says.

And that's when I realize she isn't the only new person in the room. An older couple is hovering just behind her, looking at us with curious and slightly bemused expressions. Beyond them, the rest of the house is alive with activity, people walking in, carrying things up the stairs and down the hall into the kitchen. A man who looks remarkably similar to Noah passes through the living room carrying a box of wrapped presents. Same jawline. Same hair color. He must be a brother.

Finally, all the pieces click into place in my brain. The couple right in front of us must be Noah's parents. Everyone else—that's the rest of his family.

All the Hawthornes are home.

"What happened to Italy?" Noah asks, and I allow myself the momentary distraction of how raspy and sleepy his voice sounds first thing in the morning. I tuck it away as yet another thing I love about him.

"Italy was great," a second man says from the entrance to the dining room. I spin around to see him and suck in a little gasp. Because it's Flint Hawthorne. *Flint. Hawthorne.* Oscar winner. Sexiest man alive. *The* Flint Hawthorne. "But *someone* started talking about how Christmas didn't feel like Christmas if we weren't all together," he continues. "So here we are." He looks over at Noah. "Hey, Noah. Good to see you, man." Then he looks over at me. "Megan, right? Nice to finally meet you."

The fact that I do not freak out over the very casual way he greets me is something I will always be proud of. "Yeah. Nice to meet you too."

"You guys did not have to come home for me," Noah says.

"Don't believe Flint," Olivia says, her voice low and conspiratorial. "You were an easy excuse, but the villa he rented for us was *not* a villa. It was honestly awful. Giant castle. Stone walls. Absolutely *freezing*. We mostly came home because we were all so tired of being cold all the time."

"So...you're complaining about staying in a castle in Italy?" Noah asks

"See? Thank you," Flint says. "It was a nice place."

"Fine. It was nice," Olivia concedes. "It was also frigid."

The older woman standing behind Olivia steps around her and sits down on the chair perpendicular to the couch. "Can we talk about what's really important?" she says, her gaze shifting to me. "Noah? Can you introduce us?"

I find myself sitting up a little taller, hoping against hope that my makeup isn't smudged down my face and my hair isn't a complete mess.

Noah clears his throat, then reaches over and takes my hand, giving it an encouraging squeeze. "This is Megan Sheridan. Olivia hired her to stay here and look after the farmhouse while everyone was gone. Megan, this is my mom, Caroline, and that's my dad, Graham. You saw Spencer walk through a minute ago, and I assume my other brothers are around here somewhere." Something loud clatters in the kitchen. "Along with everyone else."

"It's so nice to meet you," I say to Noah's parents. "I look forward to getting to know you both."

Caroline's expression is warm and kind. She and Noah have the same blue eyes, and her short gray hair is cut into a sleek bob. She reaches over and takes my hand, giving it a gentle squeeze. "It's lovely to meet you too."

"Have you guys had a nice week together?" Olivia asks, her expression beyond obvious.

Noah shoots me a knowing grin, then he rolls his eyes and points at his cousin. "You're lucky this worked out as well as it did."

She grins. "So it did work out?"

Noah looks at me, blue eyes sparkling. "Yeah. I really think it did."

AN HOUR LATER, I'm showered and dressed in clean clothes and feeling much more human.

I don't see Noah anywhere yet, and I still haven't officially met the rest of his extended family, so I hover awkwardly at the entrance to the living room, unsure what to do with myself. But then Caroline sees me and immediately stands and hurries over.

She pulls me into a hug. "You must be so overwhelmed," she says, her tone warm and gentle.

"A little," I say, "but I love it too. All of this is wonderful."

"Do you have a big family?" she asks.

"Just one brother, so it's nothing like this."

"Oh dear," she says. "You'll need some time to get used to us then. But trust me. It'll get easier. Are you hungry? You look like you need to eat."

After all the cheesecake last night, I'm not sure I should eat before next Tuesday. But then the smell of bacon hits my nose, and my stomach lets out a low grumble.

Caroline laughs. "Definitely hungry then. Come on. I'll introduce you to everyone."

The dining room is full of people, but still no Noah, so I stick with Caroline, smiling and nodding and saying hello as she runs down the list of Noah's siblings and cousins.

There's Olivia, of course, whom I already met. Then her husband, Tyler, and their kids, Asher and Maggie. Lennox and Tatum—the chefs of the group—are the ones making breakfast. I meet Flint's son, Milo, and his wife, Audrey, who is expecting another baby. Then there's Perry and his wife, Lila. Their son Jack is the oldest of the grandkids. Brody and Kate are sitting together in the dining room with their daughter, River, and then, of course, there are Noah's brothers, Mason, Spencer, and Will. Graham's brother and sister-in-law, Ray and Hannah Hawthorne, are in the kitchen serving up plates, which means the only two missing from the group are Noah and his father, Graham.

"He's outside," Caroline says, clearly reading my expression. "Talking to his father, believe it or not."

"Oh, that's good," I quickly say. "I'm so glad."

She narrows her gaze, studying me, like she's trying to discern how much I know.

I lift my shoulders in a shrug. "We've done a lot of talking this week."

This makes her eyebrows lift. "Noah has?" She lets out a chuckle, then loops her arm through mine. "Oh, we need to keep you around. You might just be a miracle worker."

Five minutes later, I'm seated at a table next to Olivia with a plate of pancakes and bacon and fresh fruit. The breakfast looks pretty typical, but when I take my first bite, it's all I can do not to moan out loud. These are not your average pancakes. "Oh my gosh," I say. "These are amazing."

"I know, right?" Olivia says. "I swear, Lennox puts crack in his food."

"Seriously. These are the best pancakes I've ever eaten. Why are they so different?"

"It's malted milk powder," Tatum says as she sits down across from me with her own plate. "Plus, he separates the egg whites and whips them before he puts them into the batter."

"Like I said," Olivia says. "Basically crack."

"Claimed by someone who has exactly zero experience with crack," Will says from the table beside us. I think it's Will? He's the youngest of Noah's brothers, but this one might be Spencer, who is one brother up.

"Stop nitpicking," Olivia says. "I'm just saying the food is good. Lennox?" she calls into the kitchen. "Your food is great!"

"Thanks, Liv," he calls back. "Stop telling people I cook with drugs."

Everyone laughs, but my heart is only halfway in it. The other half is outside with Noah, hoping against hope that the conversation with his father goes well.

"So, do you completely hate me?" Olivia asks. "I swear I really did need someone to be at the farm. But when Summer told me she knew of someone who might want the job, she gave me your name, I looked you up, and I just had this feeling."

"You looked me up?"

"Totally creepy Instagram stalking," Olivia says. "I don't even know what it was. Just something about your vibe that made me think Noah would totally fall for you."

"Wait, are you and Noah like...a thing?" I look up to see a *different* brother staring at me. This one is definitely Mason—the one right next to Noah in age.

"Um, I mean, it's only been a week, but..."

"You don't owe him any explanation," Caroline says, glaring at her son. "Mason can mind his own business until his brother is ready to talk about it. That goes for the rest of us too."

I smile into my plate as I fork up another bite of pancakes. It's more than a little overwhelming to have all of these people interested in my personal life, but it's also kind of amazing. No one is judging or being critical even when they're teasing each other. It's very clear they are only interested because they love each other.

I've spent the past few days imagining a life with Noah, but right now, my thoughts shift to a life with *all* the Hawthornes. With nieces and nephews and more cousins than I can count. Aunts and uncles all rooting for us—for *me*.

Just then, I hear the sound of the back door opening, then closing again. I put down my fork, waiting and watching as footsteps move through the kitchen. It takes a minute; there are muffled men's voices—maybe he's greeting Lennox? But then, finally, Noah appears in the dining room. I watch as he quickly scans the crowd. As soon as his eyes land on me, he smiles, a full, glorious smile that makes my heart climb into my throat.

"Oh, he's got it bad," Caroline says. She looks over at Olivia. "Did you see that smile he just gave her? When does he ever smile like that?"

"You're welcome," Olivia says, like she's incredibly proud of herself.

Noah sits next to me while he eats, but there are so many people, so many conversations going on at once, that we don't really have an opportunity to talk. I love the energy and the laughter, but by the time the dishes are nearly done and everyone is gathering in the living room to open presents, I'm itching for some alone time with Noah.

He must be feeling the same way because when I pass through the kitchen to put an empty glass in the sink, he catches me on my way out, wrapping an arm around my waist and tugging me into his bedroom.

I let out a gasp of surprise as Noah closes the door, then pins me against it, his body a warm, delicious weight. "Hi," he says softly, then he lowers his lips to mine.

Noah's kiss is soft and tender and exactly what I want, and I melt into him, the stress of meeting so many new people quickly draining away.

"I've been wanting to do that all morning," he says when he finally breaks the kiss.

"Hmm. You won't get any complaints from me."

"How are you?" he asks. "I know this wasn't the Christmas morning either of us expected."

"No, but it's good. Your family is amazing."

His expression softens. "Yeah. They're pretty great."

"How was your conversation with your dad?" I ask.

"Good," Noah says. "Hard. But not as hard as I thought it was going to be."

I lift a hand to his cheek, running my palm over his beard. "Good work."

"I assume you met everyone?"

"I did. I even learned that Olivia stalked my Instagram profile. Did she tell you that?"

His eyebrows lift. "Should we be flattered she went to so much effort?"

"I think…yes," I say as I tug him a little closer. "It means she loves you and she wants you to be happy."

Noah presses a line of kisses along my jaw, inching closer and closer to my lips. "I don't remember the last time I've been this happy," he says. "I'm not sure I ever have been."

"Me neither. It makes me sad to think about leaving this place. It's wild to think I've only been here a week, and yet I already love it like it's mine."

"Yeah," Noah says, giving me a pointed look. "I know the feeling."

I suck in a breath, heat flooding my cheeks as the full meaning of Noah's words sinks in. "Noah," I say softly.

"I'm not going to say it," he says gently. "Not yet. But I'm on the way there, Megan. I'm falling. I probably *will* love you a lot sooner than later."

I close my eyes for a brief moment, willing myself to keep breathing. "Yeah, me too," I manage to say, but as the words come out, I wonder if they're a lie. If the way my heart is feeling right now is any indication at all, then I'm already there.

We kiss for a long time after that, long enough that I start to worry his family might get the wrong impression.

"We're going to make your family talk if we stay in here much longer," I say.

"Let them talk," Noah says. "I can take it."

I swat at his chest. "Maybe you can, but I've known your mother all of two hours. And she knows I've only known *you* a matter of days."

Noah grumbles something I can't understand as he pulls me even closer, burrowing his nose into my neck.

"What was that?" I say as I settle my hands around his waist. I'm talking a big game here, but the truth is, as long as he keeps this up, I'm powerless to stop him.

He presses a kiss into the curve of my neck, just above my collarbone. "I said you're probably right, even if I don't particularly feel like sharing you with my family."

I smile and bite my lip. "We still have time. Lots of it, I hope. Assuming I get a job. And find a place to live. And manage to move all my stuff from New York down to Charlotte."

"I'll help you move," Noah says. "You said I should visit the city, so I'll come up. Visit. Then help you move down."

"I would love that. But I have to get the job first."

"About that." Noah leans back and pulls out his phone. "I didn't expect her to respond on Christmas, but she did, and it's good news." He taps on his phone for several seconds before holding it out to me.

I swallow, my heart suddenly pounding in my chest. "It's good news?"

He grins. "Very good."

I take the phone, hands trembling, and start to read.

Hey! Merry Christmas! Great to hear from you. Sorry for responding on a holiday, but I'm working today anyway, so I thought I'd take a quick look while I'm here. I've been so behind on hiring, but I pulled Megan's application, and she looks like a great candidate. Her letters of recommendation are solid. She'll still need approval by two other coordinators, but I don't see that being an issue. I'll keep you posted, and I hope to see you back around here soon. - Mel

"Oh my gosh," I say as I look up at Noah. "Is she saying what I think she's saying?"

"I mean, it's not a done deal," he says. "But I think it will be."

I throw myself into Noah's arms, ignoring the slight pain in my shoulder as he picks me up, spinning me around before lowering me back to the ground. "Thank you," I say. "I almost feel guilty that it took a personal connection to get the job, but I'm so excited to have it, I don't even really care."

"Don't feel guilty," Noah says. "Personal connections get people jobs all the time. Knowing someone who knows someone. That's not a bad thing."

I lean up and kiss him. "You didn't have to help me though. It means a lot to me that you did."

"Don't let it go to your head," he teases. "My motives were purely selfish."

"They were, were they?"

"Hmm," he says. "I really didn't love the idea of flying all the way up to New York just for this." He leans down and gives me a bone-melting kiss, and I forget, at least for a moment, that there's anyone else in the house at all.

Eventually, we make our way to the living room. There are only a couple of children old enough to unwrap presents, but the ones who are are sitting on the rug in front of the couch, surrounded by their parents, smiling and laughing as they experience the magic of Christmas.

Someone has built a fire in the fireplace, and it looks like a game of Trivial Pursuit is about to start at one of the tables in the dining room.

Now, more than ever, even more than I was when the Petersons showed up, I'm glad we worked so hard to decorate the farmhouse. Though, on second thought, I'm not sure it would have mattered to the Hawthornes.

I get the sense that for them, the most important part of any holiday isn't the location or the decorations or about having everything look picture perfect.

It's about being together. About taking care of each other.

Noah steps up beside me and slips an arm around my waist, tugging me into his side. "Are you good?"

I look up and smile. "Perfect."

I know enough about life to understand that things won't always feel perfect. But there is a sense of certainty right behind my ribs that's growing stronger by the minute. With Noah by my side, life won't need to be perfect—we'll just need to be together.

Weathering the storms. Enduring the sorrows so we can better appreciate the joy.

"I wish I'd gotten you something for Christmas," I say.

Noah leans down and presses a lingering kiss to my lips. "I already have exactly what I want."

Epilogue

"THE NEW NURSES ARE TALKING ABOUT YOUR MAN AGAIN," Maren says as she steps behind the desk at the PICU nurses' station.

"You say *new nurses* like I am not also a new nurse," I say as I work my way through my charting.

"You've been here six months," Maren says. "You aren't new. At least not as new as they are." She drops into a chair next to me and reaches for her iPad.

Maren is my closest friend at Northvale General and has been since my first day. She's funny and chill and easy to work with and was hugely instrumental in helping me learn the ropes, so she has my undying loyalty just for that. But she is possibly a tiny bit obsessed with relationship drama. Hers. The other nurses on the floor. Mine—even when I really don't have any.

"Let them talk," I say. "It doesn't mean anything."

She huffs. "It doesn't annoy you even a little bit? That they're brainstorming reasons to sneak down to the ER to catch glimpses of Dr. McHottyPants?"

"Is that really what they call him?" I say, feeling more amused than annoyed. It's not like they actually stand a chance with the man. I'm the one wearing his engagement ring. Well, not currently. It's a hazard at work, so I leave it at home whenever I'm at the hospital. But I know it's mine. I know *he's* mine. I can't fault them for finding him handsome.

"It's exactly what they call him," Maren says. "And I really, really think you should let them know to keep their eyes to themselves."

"I can't stop them from looking, Mare."

She rolls her eyes. "Trust me. If you had heard the kinds of things they were saying, you would feel differently."

I close out my last patient's chart and stand, pressing my hands into the small of my back to stretch. "I think you just like drama."

"Or maybe I just want you to rub it in their faces a little that he's yours."

"Like I said," I repeat. "You just like drama."

"And you love me for it!" she calls as I head down the hall.

I've got a ten-year-old patient named Lily who will hopefully be moving to the stepdown unit today, which is a big deal. She was Noah's patient first, after she came into the ER critically injured in a car accident, and things were pretty touch and go for a while. Even though Noah is no longer overseeing her care, he'll be excited to hear about her progress.

I glance at my watch, wondering if I'll be able to run downstairs to see him during my next break. Before I can look back up, an arm is around my waist, and suddenly I'm in a supply closet, my fiancé's arms holding me against his chest.

"Where did you come from?"

He leans down and kisses me long and hard. We've been working opposite shifts lately, so we haven't seen much of each other. "I missed you," Noah says, pulling me close enough to press a kiss against the curve of my neck. "This weekend can't get here fast enough."

I sigh and lean closer, tilting my head to give Noah better access to more of my skin. As soon as my shift ends on Friday, we're driving over to Silver Creek to spend the weekend at Stonebrook and finally try Lennox's restaurant. I'm excited to see the farm in the summertime and visit the goats, but mostly I'm just excited to have thirty-six uninterrupted hours with Noah.

"Hey, Lily is moving into the stepdown unit today," I say, and Noah lifts his head.

"That's great news."

"Yeah. I thought you'd think so." I lift my hands and wrap them around each of his biceps, pressing up on my toes to kiss him one more time. "It's nice to see you in the middle of the day like this, but it's dangerous having you on my floor."

"Yeah? Why is that?"

"The new hires are calling you Dr. McHottyPants."

He rolls his eyes. "Oh, geez."

"I think it's funny," I say. "I mean, you are. So…"

"But do they know we're engaged?"

"How would they know? I can't wear that ridiculous rock at the hospital."

"You could tell them," Noah says. "It would at least shut them up."

"You sound like Maren," I say. "And I barely even know them. They'll figure it out eventually."

Noah frowns and lets out an endearing grumble. "I don't want anyone calling me Hottypants but you."

"It's Dr. McHottyPants. And too bad, buddy. You can't walk through the hospital looking like you and not cause a reaction."

He leans against the supply shelf behind him and pulls me against him, settling his arms around my waist. "Let's talk about something different."

"Okay. Evie just sent me new pictures of the baby. He just cut a new tooth and when he smiles, he looks exactly like Alec's baby pictures."

"Send them to me," Noah says.

"I will. Now you go."

"Hmm. Let's see. Oh, you remember when you speculated that my dad sounded like he was itching to retire?"

"Is he doing it?" I ask.

"He just texted this morning. He'll stay on through the end of next month so the hospital has time to find his replacement, but then he's done. Said something about wanting to spend more time at the winery."

"Can they even call it a winery if they aren't making any wine?"

"Apparently, they're making really good grape juice, which is a start, I guess?"

"Oh my gosh, your brothers. They make me laugh."

"I don't know," Noah says. "I think they may actually be onto something. Okay, your turn. Anything else?"

This is often how we spend the first few minutes whenever we're together. Catching up on news and family business. Making sure we hit all the most important pieces when sometimes, we only have a few minutes together.

Eventually, I'll be able to pick better shifts. Work fewer nights. And we'll be able to sync our schedules more easily. But for now, we're just making it work as best we can.

"Oh! I do have one more thing," I say. "I know it seems totally ridiculous to make this work right now, but I've been sort of maybe a little bit stalking this one particular dog rescue and...there is a puppy there that I think would be perfect for us."

"Megan," Noah says. "A puppy?"

"I know. I know! But you just have to look." I pull my phone out of my pocket and pull up the Hope Acres website, quickly scrolling to find the puppy's pictures. "Her name is Holiday, after Billie Holiday, which I think makes her extra special, and just...look at her cute face." I hand Noah the phone, watching as he studies her, his eyes growing just soft enough that I can already tell he wants her. "She's mostly poodle, so she doesn't shed," I say, "and she won't get much bigger than thirty-five pounds. And apparently, she has the sweetest disposition and she's already crate trained and they're working on her potty training and I really, really want her."

Noah sighs. "You can't tell me that. Because you

know I can't say no when you want something, but Megan...we can't get a puppy right now."

"But we can," I say. "I talked to Mel this morning, and she all but guaranteed I'll be off night shift by the beginning of next month. We will have so much more time together after that. And I'll have more time to be with Holly."

"You've already given her a nickname?"

I grin. "It's cute, right?"

His shoulders drop and he shakes his head. "I don't know what I'm going to do with you."

"So...we can go see her this weekend? She's in Lawson Cove, which is only an hour away from Silver Creek."

Noah breathes out a highly exaggerated, long-suffering sigh. "Yes," he says with a grin. "We can go see her."

I throw myself into his arms, then pull back, taking his face in my hands so I can kiss him thoroughly. Far more thoroughly than I usually would in the hospital, but he definitely earned it. If I were on an actual break, I might be tempted to lock the closet door and—

"I have to get back to work," Noah growls, his voice raspy enough to make my blood heat.

"I know," I say with a sigh. "Me too. I'll see you tonight?"

He shakes his head no. "Alder called out, so I'll probably be here until tomorrow morning. But Friday is the day after that and then..." He kisses me one more time. "Then I'm all yours."

When we step out of the supply closet, I expect Noah to go one direction while I go the other, but he surprises me when he threads his fingers through mine and walks me all the way back to the nurses' station. The two new hires are there now, as well as Maren, who watches us approach with wide eyes.

Noah stops right in front of the desk and turns me to face him, then lifts his hands to my cheeks and kisses me right there in front of everyone.

It's not like we keep our relationship a secret. We've filed all the appropriate paperwork with HR. Checked all the boxes to make sure we're keeping things above board. But we don't exactly flaunt it either. Noah is a very private person, and I love him enough to do whatever makes him most comfortable.

So this is very uncharacteristic.

When he pulls away, his eyes sparkle with humor as he says, "I love you, fiancée. I'll see you at home."

I press my lips together to keep from laughing as he casts a pointed look toward the nursing station, then turns and heads toward the elevator. As I watch him walk away, I gotta say, the way he fills out those scrubs, he really *is* Dr. McHottyPants.

When I turn back to the nurses' station, the two new nurses are staring at me with wide eyes. "We didn't..." one of them starts.

"If you heard us talking," the other says. "We didn't know."

"And we wouldn't have," the first one says. "If we had known."

"You're totally fine," I say with the warmest smile I can muster. "Don't even worry about it. Just...maybe stick to calling him Dr. Hawthorne?"

"Right. Absolutely," the first one says.

I appreciate how readily they agree, so I decide not to tell them that Dr. McHottyPants is my new favorite nickname for my fiancé.

The End

Acknowledgments

If this is your first Jenny Proctor book, welcome! How to Kiss on Christmas Morning is a stand alone novella, but, as you might have guessed, the Hawthorne family already exists in the Jenny Proctor book world. My How to Kiss a Hawthorne Brother series chronicles the loves stories of brothers Brody, Lennox, Perry, and Flint. The series is complete, so I hope you'll check them out! The heroine in this story, Megan Sheridan, is also connected to another book. She's the main character's younger sister in When Alec Met Evie—the sister/best friend in the "best friend's brother" trope. I love writing my novels in one giant connected world, adding tiny crossovers wherever I can. There was actually one MORE right at the very end of the epilogue in this book. If you missed it, go hunting! I'm sure you'll find it!

As far as acknowledgements go, I feel like I thank the same people over and over. Which, what an amazing problem to have, right? That I get to work with such incredible people to bring my books to life. My critique partner, Kiki, as always. My editor and sister, Emily. My assistant, Kristina. I don't think I could survive without any of you.

I have to thank Sonia, who drew the most incredible cover art for this book and truly brought my characters to life. And of course, my daughter Lucy who is about to graduate from nursing school herself. She was the reason I put Megan in nursing school when I wrote When Alec Met Evie, and she was a tremendous resource in helping me figure out the timing of licensing exams and graduation and all the things that nurses think about when they're just starting out. Thanks for sharing all your knowledge, Lu. You're going to be an AMAZING nurse.

And to you, my readers, who deal with my ever changing release dates, who smile and nod as I say "Soon!" on social media over and over again, THANK YOU for your patience. For hanging with me. For being excited to read no matter when I throw you a book. You guys are the very best. I've said it before and I'll say it again. I couldn't do this job without you.

Love in Bloom

Oakley Island Romcoms

Eloise and the Grump Next Door

Merritt and Her Childhood Crush

Sadie and the Badboy Billionaire

Other Novels

The Christmas Letters

Her Last First Date

Just One Chance

Love at First Note

Wrong For You

Mountains Between Us

The House at Rose Creek

About the Author

Jenny Proctor is an award-winning author of more than twenty romantic comedies and an Amazon bestseller.

She began her career in publishing in 2013; her writing has been a constant since then and is now her full-time focus, but in the past, she spent several years as the owner and managing editor of Midnight Owl Editors and as the chair of the Storymakers Conference. Wired for relationships, Jenny loves public speaking, teaching, and building lasting connections.

Jenny lives in the mountains of Western North Carolina, a place she considers one of the loveliest on earth. She loves to hike with her family and spend time outdoors, but she also adores lounging around her home, reading great books or watching great movies and, when she's lucky, eating delicious food she did not have to prepare herself.

To learn more, find Jenny online at www.jennyproctor.com.

www.ingramcontent.com/pod-product-compliance
Lightning Source LLC
Chambersburg PA
CBHW010743310726
48971CB00010B/2925